About the author

Hailing from Dehradun and presently settled in Bangalore, Arvind Parashar has been a corporate leader in various firms like GE, Dell and Genpact. He decided to give a break to his corporate career and pursue his passion for writing. Arvind has walked a narrow path to reach where he is today. He had to sacrifice a lot, including his job, to ensure he can chase his dream without any problems. A self-made man, today Arvind is happy that his hard work and effort are bearing fruit. His first novel was a Crossword bestseller that won many hearts. His second novel *Messed Up! But All For Love* was loved by discerning readers across the country. The first part of the *Messed Up!* trilogy, it was followed by *Lost in Love,* which went on to win many hearts. *All You Need is Love* is the final part of the trilogy and promises to be a thrilling, electrifying read.

Arvind is also a philanthropist and a motivational speaker. He has addressed students and corporates across the country during various sessions and literary festivals. Arvind is a crusader for education and support for intellectually disabled children. Arvind is also a painter and enjoys painting in his spare time. He plans to do an exhibition of the same in the near future.

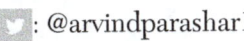: /arvindparasharauthor : @arvindparashar1

: @arvind.parashar : www.arvindparashar.com

Praise for the book

"India's first romantic-thriller trilogy... deals with various aspects of relationships."

– The Telegraph

"Sprinkled with humour... roller-coaster ride of thrilling romance."

– The Times of India

"...draws inspiration from real life instances."

– The Hindu

"...explores new age friendships and relationships."

– Deccan Chronicle

All You Need is Love

ARVIND PARASHAR

Srishti
PUBLISHERS & DISTRIBUTORS

Srishti Publishers & Distributors
Registered Office: N-16, C.R. Park
New Delhi – 110 019
Corporate Office: 212A, Peacock Lane
Shahpur Jat, New Delhi – 110 049
editorial@srishtipublishers.com

First published by
Srishti Publishers & Distributors in 2019

Printed at Repro Knowledgecast Limited, Thane

To my mom and dad.

Acknowledgements

There is nothing I could do in writing, if I did not have you. Yes, you – my dearest reader friends.

This yet another raw story turned into a novel only and only because of my editor – Stuti. You are truly blessed with this art of giving the book shape and form that readers deserve. Also, Pushpanjali, I thank you for reading and refining the manuscript at the very first stage.

Arup – thanks for being my lovely publisher.

Jayanta da – thanks for always blessing me.

The first poem in the book, 'The Realms of Conjugal Bliss', has been written specially for this romance thriller by Vandita Dharni.

Two poems in the book have been written by Dhanya Nair.

A note from the author

This is the concluding part of the romance thriller series. Book one – *Messed Up! But All For Love* and book two – *Lost in Love* have been loved by you all. I am hoping you love this one as well. There are some new characters in this book.

Lost in Love revolves around the college life of Neil and Gauri, whereas *Messed Up! But All For Love* deals with their middle age.

All You Need is Love progresses to the next level.

Hope you enjoy the thrilling experience this book offers.

Disclaimer

Do not lose your senses while having alcohol with the opposite sex. If you do and end up with adventures to share, then let an author know and see your life in the form of a book. Though, the author is not promoting this paradox in any way.

Prologue

Life brings about a variety of shades every day. Just as nature brings different seasons. Within those seasons, you have stormy days, rainy ones, hot days and cold chilly ones. You may not like some, however you can't necessarily avoid them. So is true with life – no shade can be dodged or neglected. The sooner we learn to accept that, the better it is. Eventually, it is a learning process, and it all boils down to learning and the mental adoption of it. With experiences, we learn. But then, a bigger question is, what gives us strength that keeps us going? A typical answer to that is, no matter how strong you are, it is unlikely that you can do it all by yourself. You need someone to be with you. Someone who can withstand all the seasons happily. Someone who can be by your side. And often, that someone becomes extremely special to you. That person is the one you fall in love with. You begin to take care of that someone and that someone reciprocates. That someone helps you restore your confidence when your chips are down. That one person in your life can change yours. For anything good that can happen to you, for you to be happy and successful, always remember, that to make it possible, all you need is love.

The Realms Of Conjugal Bliss

The leathery horizon beckons
The starry maze to blur their sparkle,
The gentle breeze wafts the petrichor
As the air is ripe with ecstasy.
Steals a silvery moonbeam
Through the haven of bliss.
Warm fires igniting their desires
As they savour the ocean of love.
The faint music sways their bodies
To its rapturous melody.
He delves into the depths
Of ambrosial wine she offers.
Their eyes gazing steadily
Exploring each other,
While their lips engage in a passionate kiss,
Luring them into an amorous seduction.
Their feverish bodies entwine
For an escape from the mundane
Into the realms of conjugal bliss.
A sanctum of eternal love.
A love that has the seal of heaven
The promise of forever.

La Habana

That was some speed. Fiercely throttling and wildly talking to the winds. Anything between 100-110 miles an hour. Like they were being chased down by cops for a crime. For a moment, one would imagine that if it increased any further, the Lamborghini might even take off into the air. That would have been one of a kind type of take-off from the narrow roads of Havana. And a first for the Lamborghini, or any other kind of vehicle. Quite a fascinating thought, just like the occupants of this beast.

It was dark and the headlights milked the roads. The lights falling on the road were swaying due to the winding course. The trees on the sides blocked the illumination. And that did not seem to matter to the couple occupying this high end machine. The road from the stadium to old Havana and the nearby villages was curvy with twisted turns. The adventurous couple mostly believed in taking to the road less travelled, quite literally.

"Wooohooooo… woohooooo!" screamed Gauri, as she crossed the 120 miles per hour mark, her last peak speed.

As she looked to her right, Neil sat upright with his eyes closed and put his hands on Gauri's lap. He wore a black suit with a crisp white shirt and a red slim tie with his top button loosened. Gauri was dressed to the nine in high end fashion. She wore a white dress that her friend Ritu Bahl, a well-known fashion designer in India, had made for her. They were returning from the Aerosmith concert, and the experience had made them nostalgic. About six years ago, in a different setting, they had come to Cuba for a vacation. They loved this place. This time around, a few things had changed. Neil was venturing into multiple businesses, and one of the investment hubs for him was Havana. Also, the way they had decked up made quite a mark which was significantly different from last time around. Even though Neil kept a low profile, there was still a huge chance that someone would have requested them for a media bite and hence it was always in them to be in their best attire. Havana as a city had a memorable history attached to their lives.

Before they could swap driving roles, Gauri parked the car on the side. She gave a long peck to Neil on his cheeks. She put her arms around him and it seemed like they would never leave each other. The wind troubled the kiss as Gauri's long brown hair blew between their faces. Neil left no opportunity to caress his sweet wife, while she didn't waste any moment to be loved by her man.

"Damn, these memories! This is the place that got us closer again. Remember my letter for you? Remember that night I fought with Srinya? That was literally a fist fight. Alas!"

Srinya was the daughter of a top cop who was taking revenge on some other couple, Drishti and Somesh. However, Neil got embroiled in the controversy. He was misunderstood by Gauri, but later things had got sorted out. That did bring the couple closer, but it was never easy.

"I still have that letter, darling. I still have all those lovely memories. What a time we had, minus whatever transpired with Drishti and Srinya."

"Let's not talk about that stupid woman. Let's only talk about us and more of us," Gauri said meticulously as she sat just on the side of red Lambo. It was pleasantly serene, misty, and most of all, romantic. The romance was driven by the beauty of the connection they shared and with the moon and stars and breeze and landscape – the whole of the universe. It all spelt love and happiness. That is how anyone would perceive. They were video recording these moments, intermittently capturing some still photos on the phone.

Gauri stretched her hand out as she stood erect, put her right hand on Neil's shoulder, pulled him towards herself and said gently in his ears, "Who would have thought we'll be here after half a decade for a vacation so peacefully, happily and dream of our small little world all over again! Tell me if you ever thought so. Neil, this place has given us sweet and bitter memories, and I swear I never ever thought we would come here again. And also, I am keeping my promise alive of always making love to you, despite having a baby now."

Neil held her face with his palms and softly kissed her, "Yes love, nor did I. If it were not for Alicia and her amazing husband Sreedhar's invite, we wouldn't have come here that easily. The whole business proposition also triggered because of them. You know, I wanted to explore Africa with you this time. But these guys are really sweet. Though they are distantly related to Tom, not for once did these guys make us feel out of place," Neil continued to talk while looking into her eyes that reflected love and only love.

"Haha Neil, Africa? And precisely, Cape Town? Ahem… sorry, I was just kidding," said Gauri with a wide grin.

"Not that part of the country, honey. And I know you are pulling my leg over that bitch, Rachel. I just meant a safari and the desert and all of that," Neil said with slight embarrassment. The mention of the port town could have brought a greater degree of discomfort, had this been a few years ago. However, now it was all in humour. Again, that is how it was perceived. If there was something else seething inside the couple, that was not shown or known yet.

Gauri casually took a few selfies in the quaint and picturesque backdrop as they both blew kisses in the phone camera and Panasonic Lumix GH5A camcorder. Before they could change their seat positions and get inside the car, Neil sent the photos and some of the recordings to his best friend for years, Tom.

The car took to the speed of 80 mph in a few seconds and that's where Neil put it on cruise mode. He pulled the windows down. They were about fifteen miles away from their destination. Neil glanced at his watch, waved at Gauri and the text back from Tom caught his attention. The phone beeped as it received a few more texts. Gauri asked Neil to focus on the wheels while keeping the conversation on.

"Neil, you know I was thinking if it is really worthwhile to invest here. Do you really think it is safe?"

"Come on! It is absolutely fine. Also, we are planning to build temples for our community here, and from that standpoint, I believe we shall get huge support from the government and even the locals."

"I would only suggest you to think again and then plan."

Neil was slightly irate at this point as he suddenly felt that his wife was making a U turn in the decision they had jointly taken. Or at least was trying to discourage him from something that he was more than convinced about. He looked at her angrily and said with a heavier voice, "Listen Gauri, you have no idea how business is done. And building temples is a pious activity. I am doing it selflessly."

"Neil, you don't have to get so angry. And you very well know the whole context. It has not been easy."

In the heat of the moment, Neil suddenly realized that the car had lost control and as he applied the brakes to bring it back to the main road, it hit the side with a screech. In no time, their car was shot at with hundreds of bullets as the perpetrators raced past them. The car turtled a few times over before hitting the ugly end of the road that would have led to the fall. There was no sign of any movement after that. The mobile phone flashed with love and kisses from their daughter Neilakshi, as she was waiting for her parents' response after Tom had shown her the pics.

The car did not fall down the trench, but lay in a state of limbo. As if to add to the chaos, it suddenly began to rain. The blood that oozed out was washed away, flowing down the narrow pathway. But there were no witnesses to it yet. Few cars drove by, but the car that met with the accident and fell prey to the attack, wasn't visible, hanging halfway down the edge. Neil's body was hanging out behind the door, but Gauri was not visible at all. Nothing moved. Neither their bodies, nor their senses.

2:30 a.m.
The same day

The very responsible Alicia and Sreedhar had begun to search for them, first in the neighbourhood and then across the town. They ran from pillar to post, but to no avail. They did not want to create panic in the vicinity or across, hence kept it all hush hush. This was precisely why no phone call was made to India yet. It was an anxious and fearful night for them. After all, they were hosting Neil and Gauri for their vacation, and now they seemed to have disappeared.

"Aren't you feeling cold?"

"Yes, colder indeed. Also, my feet are frozen and even my hands are going numb," said Alicia in response to Sreedhar.

Alicia had planned to kindle a cosy fire as a lovely surprise that they had planned for the missing couple. The idea was to celebrate friendship. Like most friends do. Like friends do when they meet after a long time. After they travel thousands of miles. They did not want to be in this situation. Alicia remembered how they had cancelled the Bed and Breakfast option for the whole of the month, only so they could give their friends complete privacy and a luxurious lifestyle on their vacation. Not that Neil demanded it, but they knew it would only be unfair on their part if they did not let him feel royal the way he did back at home. After Neil was announced to be one in the five hundred richest people in India. Alicia and Sreedhar had made a long video call to offer their congratulations. It was a moment of big celebration and they had made sure to be a part of it, even if only through a video call.

And when they lit up the kindle fire, it reminded them further of the *hawan* that had taken place at Neil's house. They were fortunate to witness the same on the video call.

Alicia knew all about the rituals and cultural practices India. As she stood with her hands folded, praying to god, Sreedhar watched her and cried within his heart. He did not show as much, but he bowed from a distance. She was praying for the safety of their guests.

Neil and Gauri were more like public figures now, after their story was known to the world through the book, *Messed Up! But All For Love*. Alicia had left no stone unturned to make the book launch a grand success. The book had captivated the spirit of Cuba and true relationships.

So that's how the whole idea of travel was hatched. The widely publicized launch happened in Cuba. Gauri did the book reading at El Cafe. She was joined by Neil while Alicia hosted the event. The audience was completely enthralled and were in tears during the story telling. Thinking of it, as the moments flashed, Sreedhar finally broke down. He had been holding it back for a long while.

"I love this couple. You remember when Gauri was reading out the letter she had written for Neil during their fight? It was all in Cuba," said Sreedhar as he stood close to his wife.

This was the same fight that had erupted when Gauri had had a misunderstanding with Neil, which ended with the famous love letter from the former. The book launch had a special mention of it.

"I remember it all and I have read their story like a few times over. And don't forget, I was the one who insisted that they come here for the book launch. Look, now I am really worried. It's 3 a.m. and they are not yet traceable. We are responsible for them. Let's call the cops," said Alicia.

"And you know, I have been really thinking hard about it. Should we not call up Tom? Maybe he has some information," Sreedhar said as he reached out for his phone. Within seconds, he was on the phone with Tom.

Sreedhar knew he had to come straight to the point. There were things he wanted to ask, like how Neilakshi was doing and Mehr as well. But then it was an awkward hour. It was 3 a.m in Cuba and Tom would know that. Not that Tom would have calculated it, but he had another wall clock that was set to Cuban time.

So, no matter what prep work Sreedhar would have done, Tom would have started off the way he did, "Bro, at this hour? What's wrong with an early to bed guy?"

"Tom, did Neil call or text you?" asked Sreedhar as he tried to control his nervousness.

"What the fuck are you saying? You had to call me to ask that? Isn't he there with you?" reacted Tom.

"Looks like they made some plans, and I wanted to ask you because his phone number is not reachable, nor is Gauri's. The concert got over long ago and they are not home yet."

"He had sent me a selfie a few hours back, umm… at 11.30 p.m. your time, to be precise, and texted that they were on the way to your place. That was sent from some place near old Havana, on the way to the village. Hey, by the way, did you call the cops? You should. What the fuck man… this is terrible! Did you call the cops yet?" asked Tom in a single breath.

"No, not yet… we were… I mean we were about to," said Sreedhar.

Tom was furiously disappointed at the turn of events. He almost screamed at his buddy, "Sree, are you waiting for me to call the cops from here? Please do something asap. I am getting way too worried now."

Mehr came running to the living room, hearing her husband scream.

"Damn this place. Damn Cuba. It never works fine for any of us. Hope they aren't in any kind of trouble. God, I just hope… Where are they? Where are you both?" Tom continued to talk as Mehr looked at him with a shell-shocked expression. Suddenly, she composed herself and then put her hand on his shoulders. Like a calm pearl, she asked him to relax. Her words did give him temporary respite, for he could now think again and immediately called Sreedhar back. His phone was engaged.

Mehr called Alicia from her phone. Hers was engaged as well. Without a wait to call again, Mehr called on the landline. Nobody picked up the phone. In fact, nobody was at home. The couple had decided to leave the house. They knew the place where the picture was sent from and so they headed in the direction while calling the cops and a few friends, seeking help. Time was running out and they had a brooding sense that something was terribly wrong.

There was a heavy downpour outside. The visibility was heavily blocked. Alicia was on the wheel after she spoke with her friend. There was no news on the radio of any accident or untoward incident so far and this kept them a bit calm. Alicia returned Mehr's call. On the other hand, Sreedhar calmed Tom down, who was deeply concerned.

The rain wasn't ready to subside and the clouds thundered like never before. Their phones kept buzzing. One after the other, even resonating in their ears. Sreedhar kept looking in all directions. He was trying to spot the car. Together, they scoured the route for any clues.

In a few minutes, Dhanya called up Alicia. Dhanya was extremely close to Neil and Gauri, and was a cop. This was probably the only call that could ease the couple at such a time. Dhanya assured them of all the support and told her that the couple had a security cover and their car was bullet proof. Alicia and Sreedhar were somewhat pacified, but it still did not take their mind off the worry at hand.

Dhanya asked Alicia to not think of anything else at this point. Neither of an accident, nor an abduction. She added further that the couple might be keeping a low profile and hence would not have revealed about the security and the works.

"Alicia, do you remember if Neil or Gauri ever mentioned Srinya or Arya?" asked Dhanya.

"Damn those bitches! I read about Srinya in their book. As far as Arya is concerned, Gauri told me about her. Who can ever forget such villains? Last I heard was that Arya had left India after the college fisaco. And to the best of my knowledge, Srinya never visited Cuba. I am certain you would know more," said Alicia, while looking outside the car window.

Arya had studied with Neil and Gauri in the college. She was the daughter of an affluent political leader. Due to her drug addiction, she had landed in a complete mess and screwed her life and also the lives of Neil and his loved ones. That was about a couple of decades ago. Dhanya, being a cop, could not rule out any possible angle of crime.

"I have already spoken with the chief of crime bureau there. We had worked on an assignment together during my stint with Interpol. His name is Carlos. He is a dear friend of mine. We shall find them soon. You guys can call me anytime," said Dhanya after listening patiently to Alicia.

"Thanks, cop. You have been a blessing," said Alicia with gratitude.

In no time after the call from Dhanya, the road had a fleet of police cars. The place was lit up with flash lights and activated with blaring sirens. It was as if Obama was visiting the country. Not less in any form or manner.

Alicia pulled over for gas. The tank wouldn't have lasted more than a ten-mile distance on a freeway. The freeway was still a couple of miles away. With the fleet of vehicles causing traffic, the risk was more.

Sreedhar checked inside for the restroom. He glanced at the television set. The loud volume distracted his gaze. What he saw on the television made him tremble. He loudly shouted Alicia's name, and began to run helter-skelter, as if hell had frozen over.

The store manager ran towards Sreedhar and started talking about the incident that was being shown on the television.

"Sir, this is what they have been showing for the last fifteen minutes, and it is quite disturbing. There was a couple who was driving down from the concert area at a very high speed before the accident took place. What is most shocking is the power with which the car hit the tree. They had rammed it with such force that the bodies must have gone flying out of the window in the trench. That is why they have not been able to discover the bodies yet. I have not seen anything like this in so many years. And because of the rains, the trace is becoming increasingly difficult for them. Also considering this large fleet going to the spot, it looks to me that the people inside the car were very powerful." The store manager made all the relevant observations and presented them to Sreedhar. He did not care how his listener would feel or react. He just found his outlet to blurt out whatever he had absorbed.

Sreedhar was in no mood to pay attention to every detail. Words like 'body' and 'killed' were far from his thoughts. Alicia came running towards her husband as she could see him standing still on the spot for a real long time. She saw the news and stood frozen. Then she held her husband's hands, who was shivering. Despite guarding themselves against anything negative, being positive and hopeful, the couple was kind of getting prepared mentally to some extent for a long, dreadful night.

As the couple went back to their car, they turned the radio set on. It was the same news. The news channels were constantly talking about a couple who was highly influential and was probably guests of a diplomat in Cuba, who might have lost their lives tonight. Alicia and Sreedhar, both reached out to the stop button together. They just did not want to believe what they were hearing.

"You know Sree, it is just not possible. I cannot believe they are no more," said Alicia in a heavily emotional state.

"Look honey, we are only few miles away from the spot. You don't worry. I am very certain they are absolutely fine. I am not having any bad feeling right now," replied Sreedhar.

Out of further curiosity, Sreedhar turned on the radio set, not necessarily feeling the need of seeking Alicia's permission, even though he realized the news might have become more disturbing now. To their horror and dismay, the news anchor was now talking about a murder angle. There were gunshots all over the car. Alicia did remember Dhanya telling her that they had a complete security cover to themselves and the car was also bulletproof. Yet there was an attempt to kill them this way. It was hard to believe.

After thirty minutes, driving through the traffic caused by the fleet and the towing trucks and the media crew, they finally managed to get a view of the accident spot from the distance. They stood rooted, unable to comprehend the sight in front of them. What could have happened to such a lovely couple was a matter of grave concern. They had no animosity known to them, yet someone had hired goons and had them fire hundreds of bullets at the couple.

Few weeks ago

Mumbai has everything to offer that one can ever imagine. This is a known fact anyway. And this is one city that provides opportunities to both the rich and the poor. When Neil had moved here a few years ago, little would he have thought that he would own a building next to Shahrukh Khan's. There definitely was much more that Neil had achieved today. Considering what Shahrukh Khan means to India and Mumbai, it made perfect sense to him to think the way he did and be filled with pride. He stood near his window, looked at the beach right across the road in front of his house. The weather was stunning outside.

He wore a crisp white shirt, a bow tie, and steel grey trousers that were purchased from Italy earlier this year. His shoes were from London which Gauri had gifted him on his birthday. The last time Neil had worn this outfit was at the dinner hosted by the King of Saudi. The shoes were never worn before, though.

This was a familiar sight. Neil would look outside like this after he had dressed up. He had transformed into a debonair, envied by many, although he remained humble in his demeanour. At the age of forty, the age that Neil very well defied, he had appeared in all the top magazines of the world, the latest being in *Time's* top 100 most influential men on the planet. His rapid growth in the past few years was always attributed to his doting daughter Neilakshi. She was an angel in the life of the couple.

Like a daily ritual, he stood still for fifteen minutes and introspected about the previous day.

Suddenly an email distracted him. Even if he had decided not to read it, there was no way he could have chosen not to. The email carried some strong words, hard enough to put him off. Neil was flying off to America that night. He was to be felicitated with the Man of the Year award from TIME. The announcement had come only last week. The disturbing email read something like this:

'Hey Neil,

It appears to me that you have comfortably forgotten me. It is not a good sign buddy. I don't want you to forget me ever. Hahaha, I won't let you forget me. You can count your days on your fingertips and so it goes for your family. Remember all those letters from me in the past? I am the same Isabella. And I still love you, Neil. And since I cannot have you, I would send you to god soon. Hope to see you on the other side of the world.
Love,
Isabella

In the middle of all the wonderful news from the world, and so many celebratory and congratulatory messages, Neil did not know how to react to this one. Was he supposed to take the contents of the email seriously, or was he supposed to ignore them like a hate mail from any of his arch rivals?

The reaction from Neil did not last long. While he was extremely conscious that the threatening emails needed to be dealt with utter care as he had a public image, at the same time, the mention of a threat to his family shook him. He had been kind of lackadaisical earlier on, and then there had been only hand written letters and notes which he could carelessly ignore, but this time around, in the world of cyber security advancement, to send an email to one of the most influential men in the world is a real challenge and merits no ignorance whatsoever.

He called his trusted aide Vidhi on her phone. She was his Executive Assistant (EA) and quite aware of most of the events. She rose to fame after winning the best EA award at one of the global events recently. She had won it because she had all the support of this man.

The cyber cops were informed in no time. Meanwhile, Neil looked for Gauri. She was on her way to collect a packet from the garage. The driver had kept it there, and she had forgotten to get it earlier. It had arrived last week. The packet was in the name of Neilakshi, which was not observed earlier. The signature was predictably, 'Love, Isabella'. Inside the packet were pictures of Neil with his friends when they had visited Tashkent a few years ago. The back of the photographs described the situation vividly. Only very few people would have known about it. So when Gauri met Neil for breakfast, it was quite obvious that they would lose their appetites. They really did.

Neil received a call from Dhanya. "Vidhi called me this morning and said that the email had come from Tashkent. Know anyone there?"

There was complete silence. Gauri ran madly towards her phone and called up Neilakshi's school.

❖

Present day

"Neil was talking about a letter from Isabella and apparently that had come from Tashkent. It did not carry enough substance or credibility for us to take it forward. Did any of them mention this to you during their stay in Havana?" asked Dhanya. She was on call with Alicia for the last twenty minutes.

"No no, not at all. How is that connected with what has happened here? Like how?" Alicia was not completely present in the discussion with Dhanya, even though she was aware of how crucial this piece of information could be. Her focus was on the road. She had a belief that she would spot the couple somewhere. Not sure why, but she believed it. Like many of us do. We keep hope alive till we see it gone with our own eyes. Hope remains alive till we become dust.

"So, Dhanya was talking about someone called Isabella. Do you recollect any such instance when this name was mentioned?" she asked her husband.

"Is she from Havana? To me right now, the name sounds like that of a fugitive."

"I am just Googling her name. Damn, I see so many in Cuba with this name. Phew. The cops will get to it for sure. But I am not aware of any Isabella theory as far my interactions go. But I do recall that Gauri was constantly in touch with Vidhi. Since she is Neil's EA, I didn't find anything awry, but it did catch my attention."

Alicia immediately called Dhanya back. She told her about Vidhi. Dhanya remembered seeing her on a couple of occasions, especially when Neil had launched his high network program called Baaz for the Indian Air Force. That was the contract which gave him an international uplift. In fact, that was one of his first network security programs which dealt with highly sophisticated Indian Air Force systems. Vidhi was the one who had organized the event and she had done a brilliant job. When the officials from PWC had come to visit her to take an appointment with Neil, she dealt with them professionally. Dhanya had made those observations then and articulated to Neil how great his team was.

That was something beyond an EA's job. Looked like she was on the way to be promoted to a bigger role in NG Worldwide Ltd. The company was now run by Neil and Gauri and three board members. The investors were Oakhill. It was real big. The company had recently received a funding of 750 million USD. And you know it well that when you are on the roll with big projects and are on your way up, everyone bows before you like they would before the rising sun. It was like that. His staff felt the same; privileged to be part of the organization.

"I remember Vidhi quite well. Let me speak with her now, even though she was on number nine in my list of people to be spoken to. And I am only done with two. And remember to be alert and let me know if you find anything."

"There is no clue about where the bodies of the couple are, and it's almost time for the sun to bloody show up," said Carlos in angst. He seemed frustrated. The cops in Havana had dealt with crimes in the past, but this one had an international impact, and hence more pressure.

"The chief is extremely upset right now. This will make global headlines according to him," replied one of the cops as he scanned the place. Fortunately, the rain had stopped. The entire area was cordoned off. The media had decided to stay till the news remained warm. As the clock struck six, the sun came up mildly. The clouds did appear dark, with rays glistening through its maze intermittently. Every stroke of the sun gave relief to the rescue team. And an added hope.

Three gruelling hours into the operations, and nothing had worked out as yet. Alicia and Sreedhar were about half a mile away from the location. The Caribbean town had had accidents in the past – it had a history of drug cartels and murders, however nobody there, at least who was talking about it, remembered anything like this ever since they started being aware.

The chief was questioning the private security of the couple. Carlos was leaving no stone unturned to be personally involved in the matter. He was being secretive too. When he had visited India back in 2014, it was Dhanya who had ensured he was being taken care of. He was hosted and shown the country. He had made several friends in India, and Dhanya remained his special friend ever since.

Back at the scene, even though it was Carlos's duty to ensure the case gets solved, but for his rank, he wasn't needed to be on the site, running around and talking to people. He felt so connected to Neil and Gauri that despite being a cop, he shed tears the moment he reached the wreckage site. He had seen many accidents and shooting incidents in his career as he moved up the ranks, and based on what he observed, there was no way according to him that they would've survived. After he had done his questioning with the folks he intended to, he called up Dhanya.

What followed was an emotional exchange of words.

"I've got my flight tickets, Chief. Please do whatever it takes, but find them alive. There are many hearts connected with this couple and I just don't want to believe they aren't alive. Till you see them otherwise, don't lose hope and don't say that they haven't survived, please," Dhanya broke down completely.

Carlos was numb. He was soon surrounded by the media, and had to face their questions one after the other. He was still reeling under the emotional upheaval after he spoke with Dhanya. A mild drizzle covered a layer of tears on his face, but his expressions revealed his plight. His strength helped him resume his professional demeanour in no time, thankfully. He took all the questions and committed to the media that he and his team would solve the case in the next twenty-four hours. And then he left the spot, giving instructions to the cops. Soon, the cops were joined by sniffer dogs.

There were signs of footsteps that were now visible, which suggested at least three people had stood on the ground. The distance was within the vicinity from which the gun shots had been fired at the car. From the initial inference what could be made out was that their speeding car and the couple trying to escape the shooters was what led to the loss of control. And once the car hit the tree and almost landed in the trench, the attackers got down and fired the bullets, to make sure that their target wasn't left alive. They later realized that the car was bullet proof. So they got down, and to confirm, shot more bullets. They then opened the door and threw them down the trench. There was a river flowing below. All this needed to be established for confirmation only after the forensic reports would come in.

Right now, this was what media headlines were. In India the headlines and a part of the news said:

NG Network Ltd founder Neil and wife go missing in Havana.

16 June 2018

PTI

This is extremely sad news that the nation has got today. A young business tycoon Neil and his dentist wife went missing after a fatal car accident and an attempt to kill by some alleged gangsters in Havana earlier in the night. According to Carlos, the chief of police of the city, he has never come across such a horrific accident and an attack in his career. The mystery remains till the bodies are recovered.

The day Neil was flying to America

Neil sat down in his hammock in the lawn. There were palm trees that grew in lines of ten each in half a dozen rows. There were hammocks and canopies and an artificial water body which almost seemed like a lake. It was ten times larger than the size of a commercial swimming pool. The couple would usually come here when they wanted to unwind and think and plan, or even socialize. Today, there was a fair amount of chaos. Somehow, after about a couple of hours of the arrival of the email, Neil was back to his normal form. Just like it happens in most situations, the initial news or instance of pain or joy takes time to sink in and once it does, you get used to it. Neil resumed his confident self.

Gauri, in the meantime, finished her discussion at Neilakshi's school. The day chosen by the cyber crime perpetrator was perfect. The person was well aware of everything and hence wanted to create fear in their minds. From the security standpoint, there was always a personal security cover provided to them. And that was in addition to the couple of cops that the government had provided.

Since the report was filed with cyber crime cops, the investigation had begun to figure if there was any link here. The emails of all the employees were well scanned. Vidhi and a few others were not really comfortable. From being the favourites to being the ones interrogated did not quite go down well with them.

Vidhi decided to tender her resignation and applied for immediate leave, citing reasons of ill health and personal issues. This happened the same day Neil was flying out of India.

There were several in command who would deal with the situation with ease, however to see Vidhi leaving, Neil felt quite upset. He did not call her yet and chose to keep quiet. He somehow knew that talking to her immediately might not solve anything.

He lay down soothing himself in the bright sun and listening to Jon Bon Jovi. 'Blaze of Glory' was still close to his heart as he remembered it as a teenager.

I wake up in the morning
And I raise my weary head
I've got an old coat for a pillow
And the earth was last night's bed
I don't know where I'm going
Only God knows where I've been
I'm a devil on the run
A six gun lover
A candle in the wind
When you're brought into this world
They say you're born in sin

Well, at least they gave me something
I didn't have to steal or have to win
Well, they tell me that I'm wanted
Yeah, I'm a wanted man
I'm a colt in your stable
I'm what Cain was to Abel
Mister, catch me if you can
I'm going out in a blaze of glory
Take me now, but know the truth
I'm going out in a blaze of glory
Lord, I never drew first
But I drew first blood
I'm no one's son
Call me young gun…

"Gauri, sometimes I feel, we were so much better in Guwahati, Siliguri and Pune and all those places where we were not in the news everyday," Neil said weighing his voice. He had earphones on and could still hear voices from outside.

Gauri stood beside him, slightly leaning over. She just smiled without uttering anything. Then she held him close to herself and whispered in his ears, removing the shining blue Bose earphones, "Everything is fine, darling. You just make the best of your trip. You have won the award and someone is fucking jealous of you and doesn't want you to enjoy it."

Even though she said that, Neil was kind of certain that this wasn't a business rivalry. It wasn't probable. The email scans didn't provide any lead and that helped him ascertain that to an extent. That apart, this threatening content wasn't new; the only difference was the potential or intensity of the content and that the medium had shifted from postal to email. It had been haunting him for a long time, even before he was an entrepreneur of this degree. Neil decided to let it go. Gauri's words helped him to calm down.

Neilakshi had come back early from school. The three of them spent some quality time together. Neil had stayed away from his work and just wanted be with his family.

"I wish we could also travel with you. If Neilakshi didn't have her exams, we would have come along," said Gauri as she always loved to be by her husband's side, especially at such an important awards ceremony.

Sometimes moments of happiness don't last very long. Just as Neil was recuperating from the horrors of the threats and resignation of Vidhi, the news reached him of the death of his confidante – Rahul Sood. He was an IIM Ahmedabad grad who was very aspirational and had become very close to Neil. He had played a significant role in the Air Force project. The news sent chills down his spine and he froze for a few minutes. When one of his staff shared the news, Neil hung up in shock. Within some time, the cops reached his place.

"It was suicide and we shall take some time to figure the reason. Apparently, he had left a note that nobody should be blamed. And it was in his handwriting. Yet we are digging deeper into what the issue could be," said Tambe, sub inspector, Bandra Police Station.

Tambe had stationed his cops for Neil's security. He was always an honest cop. Diligent and sharp.

Before Tambe left, he whispered something in Neil's ears, kind of dropping him some clues or cautioning him. He had some information that he subtly shared. Neil thanked him.

"Thanks Tambe ji. Please have some tea before you leave."

Tambe obliged. He told the driver to never leave the car unattended. In fact, he kind of warned the driver, "I will fuck your happiness if you ever leave the car in stray parking places without an eye. *Maar lunga main teri Deshpande, samjha?*"

Present day

It was noon. The search operations were over. A booty of a million dollars was announced for anyone who could give a clue. That was a big amount for anyone. After the announcement, almost every Cuban turned into an investigator, looking at every brown skinned Asian with suspicion. They knew if any gangster was involved, then it would mean extending their network. For once, the laid back city became a lot busier.

The media was lined up right outside Sreedhar's house. He and Alicia decided to leave from the backdoor. They were best to be avoided. Sreedhar and Tom had a long chat in the morning to find out if there was any suspicious angle that had been overlooked and needed to be shared with the cops.

On the other side, Carlos had taken his commitment to heart and did not want a delay by even a second beyond twenty-four hours to solve the case. His aim was to find them both alive. Eight hours had already passed.

Dhanya later decided to stay in town so that she could get the investigation expedited in the country too. No angle could be ruled out. When Dhanya got to know about Rahul's suicide, she spoke with Tambe who maintained that the investigations were on track. The case was still open, though. Dhanya was surprised to learn that Vidhi had gone for a holiday to a place unknown, though Dhanya was sure she'd find out eventually.

Here in Havana

Sreedhar and Alicia were finally able to escape from the rear door. An escape actually from the media. And both of them did not want to waste even a single minute sitting idle. They had to find Neil and Gauri, somehow. Anyhow. Turn by turn, they decided to talk to Dhanya and Tom. Finally they reached their store. The couple ran a watch and jewellery store in the suburbs. The staff appeared sad, as expected. Upon seeing their boss, the lady at the reception immediately switched the television off. She knew the news would turn them off completely.

"What's the latest news update, guys?" asked Alicia.

"The cops seem to be clueless, madam, but it is good that they have put a million dollars worth of reward to find them. Your friends are really big people, madam."

"Yes, indeed. But the cops have not put this award. It is the board of their company which has rightly done so," answered Alicia with a choked voice.

"Sir, someone came ten minutes ago to sell this watch. We gave him a thousand dollars for this, however, this is a Swiss Omega, so I am sure this will fetch us good money. That's a happy sale. But sir, we had a doubt. Why would he sell it for so less?"

Sreedhar was looking outside so he just said to his staffer from a distance, "Hope you haven't been fooled, Nick."

"No, sir. I know I am not good with diamonds, but watches are my forte, sir," Nick said as he walked towards his owner with the watch.

"What the fuck! Oh my… what the heck… who was the guy? I want to know everything."

Alicia looked at Sreedhar with utter surprise as she had never seen her husband swear in such a manner. She knew he was highly tensed over something. What she would discover in some time would be an absolute shocker.

"This is Neil's watch! Damn it, this is his watch. Oh gosh, give me strength O Lord…"

The couple sat astonished for a while. In complete bewilderment, Sreedhar asked Nick all the details. He pulled out the CCTV records and showed the picture of the so-called Andres who claimed to have received the watch as a gift from one of the American tourists. He found the watch useless to him and therefore came to sell it. Nick said he had forgotten to take Andres' phone number as he was distressed and distracted that morning, by the news on the television.

Sreedhar immediately informed Carlos. At this point, hope to find the couple alive was beginning to diminish. He was giving up.

"We live on a blue planet that circles around a ball of fire that is next to the moon that moves the sea, and you don't believe in miracles? They are fine. I am telling you, trust me. Trust god." Alicia was sure of her well-contained consolation.

Sreedhar spoke with Tom and told him about the situation. Tom was flying to Cuba with Mehr and Neilakshi later that night.

❖

It was a plush residence set along the lanes of coffee gardens. At some distance, one could also see the sugarcane fields. The land size was close to fifty acres and it was the government which flouted its norms then to please the occupant of this place. David More was ruling the place like a king. He was called the Pablo of the region. There was an era that completely belonged to him. However, when the Venezuelan government tightened its noose on the route that David used for drug smuggling, he tried to use Canada and Mexico to supply into America. That did not last forever, specially with the big arrest of El Chapo. For the last couple of years, the government of Cuba had also gotten very strict, because they did not want to mess up its relationship with America. David then decided to bring about a change in his operations. He ventured into steel, construction and cement business, something that Cuba was already known for, and there existed a huge space.

David's life changed after he married Arya. The same Arya who had screwed up Neil's life back in college. Infamous for drug abuse and heavy alcohol, she made quite a headline back then. She met David at Goa during her holidays. They instantly hit off and Arya moved to Cuba and married him. David soon took over from his father and expanded the drug cartel.

At present, he was still operating in a controlled manner. The money that he earned from his superficial business activities supported him to keep a clean image.

He held a huge land where he was carrying out these drug-related activities. That operated in the garb of the church. The land was provided by the government to him at a subsidised rate.

Things began to crumble a bit when the government showed a bit of shift in their attitude, as they began to invite lot of foreign investors. Countries like China, Russia and Canada always had a great business relationship. However, now it was India that was stealing the limelight.

David was not quite happy with certain events that had taken place over the last few days. He had not confided in anyone as yet, but Arya sensed it somehow.

"I have never seen you so pensive in the past. You are not talking much and kind of keeping aloof. Will you not even share it with your wife?" asked Arya as she leaned over her man.

David held a cigar between his lips, biting off the outer leaf. He had not lit it yet. Then he stood up, and held Arya's hand and in a classy style looked at the walls of the lobby area and then walked closer.

"You know, it is all our forefathers who had a dream, and they gave up everything to make that dream come true. They wanted to build Cuba into what it is today. They worked hard and we carried that legacy forward. And now, the government is trying to take our lands away. Because they want to build an industrial estate. They want to take our churches away. They have gone nuts. You think that is possible? Hahaha, they are fools if they think like this," scoffed David.

"David More, nobody can touch it and we both know that. Come, let me ease you off," said Arya as she pulled him over and made him sit on the couch.

Slowly, seductively, she took David's mind off everything else, but her body. It did the trick, like always.

Just when Arya rolled off David, making herself comfortable next to him on the couch, David received a call on his landline. The caller spoke in Russian. Arya poured him some single malt. After he kept the phone, he turned on the television to watch the news.

He stared at the headlines. He looked at Arya, gulped the drink and said while shaking his head. "What the fuck is going on?"

❖

More than ten hours had gone by. Carlos was smoking a cigar on his office terrace. The office overlooked a vast expanse of forest trees. The area was well used for commando training. He was restless that day. Irrespective of the chaos around, he had to think and keep the search operations going at war footing levels.

As he puffed away the smoke, creating spirals in the air, one of his deputies came with vital information. It is a different thing that the police station had received more than a thousand calls since morning, not giving any clues or whereabouts of the missing couple but asking the modalities of the million dollar reward.

The guests at the station were an old couple. After getting a nod from the chief, the cop made them sit and had black tea sent to them. Carlos had clearly instructed his deputy to get all the relevant info first and then update him. If he found it worthy, he'd take over and decide the further course of action. Based on the development, the deputy decided to rope in the chief.

"So, what was the approximate time when you saw them last?"asked Carlos, looking deeply into the eyes of the man, whose identity was figured. He was fondly called Juan by the family. The lady was called Cecilia. They were a charming old couple. Juan took no time to answer, "The concert got over at 12.30 in the night. It was very loud outside. Both Neil and Gauri were sitting next to us—"

Before Juan could finish, Carlos intervened, "Sir, if you don't mind, please answer only what I ask you." Then he showed him the format of the questions on his laptop. It was in sequential order. The structure was Carlos' brainchild. Last year, when there was a heist at one of the museums which housed some antiques, Carlos had his office transformed to hi-tech. With the US opening its doors for Cuba, there were many techies who were involved in crime. That is when the police got more organized and streamlined. Even the crime rate was subsiding. Carlos was aware of each and every gang in town. This incident therefore gave him a rude shock and he realized someone big was involved.

"Sure, sir. Please ask your questions and we shall cooperate," answered Cecilia on behalf of the old man. She was getting nervous.

"How was the couple behaving?" asked Carlos with a stern chief kind of look. He made it clear that he was not in to be fooling around.

"They were extremely friendly and Gauri was such a nice person. She even spoke with us in broken Spanish. We did not… oh I am sorry, please ask your next question," said Cecilia as she realized the cop was in mood to hear anything apart from what he wanted to know.

"Okay, now tell me everything that happened till you saw them last." said Carlos.

"We came out and we were surprised to see that they had armed security with them. At least eight of them. All dressed in black. In some sort of uniform. Like we see in Hollywood movies. And you would have seen too in pirated versions when we did not have much access… you know what I mean… Oh, I am so sorry for talking so much. One of them looked like Nicholas Cage," chuckled Cecilia. She was sharp in describing the scene vividly. She paused for water and then Juan continued.

"Yes sir, she is correct. They invited us to visit India. I have heard a lot about the country. I want to go there once. But we would only go with the couple. Please find them soon."

Carlos replied, "Yes, it is a beautiful country with beautiful people, and I had the privilege to be hosted by a senior cop over there. I had gone there as part of a knowledge exchange program as part of Interpol and further strengthen relationship between two countries. Their prime minister needs to visit us and I will host him. I have heard that he keeps a strong relationships with all the countries. But now I feel let down. I couldn't take care of them, how can they trust us anymore…," he continued to talk and kept walking in anger.

"Sir, you don't worry. I am sure you will find them soon."

"So what happened after that meeting of yours?" Carlos kept the questions going.

"Sir, we noticed something weird. They asked their security to let them spend some quality time alone. It was decided by them to go to the village for a midnight food festival that was meant for couples only. Mostly you would see foreign tourists going for an event like that. Afterwards, when they were leaving, I noticed there were two cars with some men in them.

"They started following the couple. Both their number plates were identical. I am forgetting exactly what the license plate was like, but it started with IS something. ISR or ISA…," Cecilia continued, with Juan interrupting in between.

Carlos had asked for all the CCTV footages, but this one in particular was missing. The one in the parking lot was working however, so at the exit gate, they could spot the men leaving. When they showed the couple their pictures on the recording tape, they confirmed that they were the same men in unison.

"Please don't leave town as we would really need your help," said Carlos swiftly.

Carlos left the station immediately after thanking the couple. There was work to be done.

Few weeks ago – Award ceremony in America

The decor was all flashy. It was one of the most coveted events held to felicitate the most powerful entrepreneurs in the world. The venue was Madison Square Garden. It was truly grand and attracted worldwide media coverage. All the prime senators were present, among the creme da la creme from the world over.

Neil was happy and overwhelmed. Dinner and drinks had just begun.

Rachel was waiting to grab the moment to strike a conversation with Neil. He had been avoiding her after their spat the previous year.

Rachel was a tall urban class high-society entrepreneur who was heir to one of the largest defense control systems company in the world. She knew the who's who in the industry and her royal lineage dated back to 1800s, when her ancestors were close to the British and dealt with liasoning in arms supply. They had ships that would ferry the same from Europe. The pay backs existed even then and the trend has continued ever since. Only more sophisticated now. She was very certain she'd grab the order for the billion-dollar deal that ended up with NG Networks.

After she had got mildly drunk, she figured her way, reached out to him and said, "The colour of my skin and size of my boobs doesn't seem to please you anymore, my charm."

"What makes you so thick-skinned, Rachel?"

"Think about it yourself. You are the one who took away my business contract and all that you did last year should have gotten me furious and vindictive forever, yet I am here with you, looking in your eyes because I know I have nothing to hide. I was and shall always be honest with you. I like you and that is what makes me thick-skinned, Neil." She was remindful in her tone.

Neil looked at her with complete surprise. He had been keeping away from her for quite some time. There was only the brief period when the two had clicked well and had taken off on a constructive course. Somehow they got on the wrong side of the course. The news about the proximity between the two had made some way into the media. When the news began to hog page 3, Vidhi had activated the PR and asked them to not publish the story. The media took a backseat. Only when one of the interns printed some pictures of them holidaying in South Africa, the media got reactivated and Vidhi ended up firing the PR and hired a London-based firm. That was a horrible time for the family. Neilakshi was in Gauri's womb then. Gauri was busy with preparations of motherhood, her dental franchise expansion and here in the middle of NG growing leaps and bounds, the media glare was bent on tarnishing his image.

"I have been craving for your love, Neil. Tell me what do you want me to do? I shall oblige. In return, just spend some time with me in my room. I am thirty and I have these fucking men ready to be mine. But I don't want them. I just want you. And you know that. Ask me, Neil. Tell me what you what."

"I just want you to give a statement in the press for once that you are a crazy psychopath."

"If you fuck me tonight, I will do that. Deal?"

"I won't ever do that."

"Never say that dear. What makes you forget Cape Town?"

"You had spiked my drink and I had trusted you."

"Real men don't lose their senses."

"So if I am not a real man, then why do you want all this from me?"

"I never said that. I said that real men don't lose senses and you were in your complete senses."

"Then why did you spike it?"

"So that I could see you pretend while you fucked me."

"I did not do anything…"

"You were almost there, out on the beach, and only that fucking intern screwed it for us. He came from nowhere. He took pics without permission and had them printed all over the South African press, including the *Sun*. They love doing it. Princess Diana wasn't spared either."

"Rachel, let me go. I don't want any unwanted attention from the press." Neil swiftly left her behind by many steps.

Rachel did not like it. Her blood was seething. She felt completely ignored and with an abrupt and unpleasant ending by Neil, she was left fretting and fuming. She was in a dilemma. If she followed Neil, the press would make sure the footage is shown. If she did not, she'd feel inundated. She was literally feeling heavy like she had lost her oxygen mask while swimming deep inside the ocean. It made her mad. She had no way to reach out to him.

Neil had smartly begun to engage with Ambanis and made it appear natural. The latter congratulated him with a warm hug. They discussed projects, the situation in the country and also about their families.

"You know, Neil, every time I travel out of the country, there are still folks from the media who are very inquisitive about the whole program stitched around the Make in India project, and everything about our country. And I have been constantly thinking that it is people like you who are bringing accolades to the nation." He sounded humble as always.

"Mukesh sir, I only wonder what makes you so humble. You are the richest man around, yet so grounded. Even at Antilla, you personally host us."

"Thank you, Neil. I owe a lot to Neeta and my children. And also to the millions of share holders. They keep me grounded."

Neil was completely in awe of the billionaire. They talked for a while longer. In some time, he looked distracted. He received a message on his phone from Gauri.

Honey, I hope you are enjoying things. There is a Facebook Live that is showing you via CNN news channel. I saw a clip where you and Rachel were talking. Please be cautious of her. And by the way, you are such a looker, man. Handsome Neil. My Neil." Gauri wrote while she continued to watch the ceremony.

Thanks my Gauri. You don't worry about Rachel, I am extremely wary of her, typed Neil as he stepped aside to avoid media cameras.

Soon they were joined by a few other folks from the gathering. The night continued amidst the glitterati.

Bryan Adams was playing live that night. The song was *Cuts like a Knife.*

Drivin' home this evening
I coulda sworn we had it all worked out
You had this boy believin'
Way beyond the shadow of a doubt, yeah
Well I heard it on the street
I heard you mighta found somebody new, yeah
Well who is he baby, who is he
And tell me what he means to you, oh yeah
I took it all for granted
But how was I to know
That you'd be letting go
Now it cuts like a knife
But it feels so right
Yeah, it cuts like a knife
Oh, but it feels so right…

Rachel went to her room in haste as soon as she exited the restroom. She had carefully decided that there was no point for her to come to the main area and then leave again. Her need to pop her sedatives was immediate as well. According to her, she was doing right. She never ever felt in her life that she had taken a wrong decision. To her, everything was her choice. The people she loved must always listen to her. That was her belief and that is when Neil happened to her. She always only wanted to be personally very close to Neil. She wanted Neil to acknowledge that whatever he was today was because of Rachel. She wanted Neil to hold her hand like a close friend. It had never started with obsession. It had started with friendship.

Rachel actually had a big role to play in Neil's initial success. However, it would be crazily stupid to imply that Neil had not put in the effort himself. He slogged a lot. Whatever Neil was today, he would have still been. Rachel was just a catalyst. When Neil was finding it hard to bag his first big contract in Cape Town, Rachel educated him on how he possibly could and did not participate herself. That avoided any coverage of sorts. However, in her heart of hearts, Rachel began to feel that Neil would seek her guidance. She had always liked him and that was the starting point without a doubt. But it was not that mad attraction for anyone. It was a normal fondness. It turned into something like needing attention when she did not get that kind of reciprocation from Neil every day. It was not practically possible, but that was what she had begun to feel and expect from Neil.

It is quite like a mother raising her children. Then, when the mother expects them to listen to her all the time and to seek her permission before anything big, kids feel that they don't need her permission any longer as they've grown up and can take their own decisions. This can lead to misunderstanding.

Here, these were two different individuals. Rachel was floored by Neil's speech at one of the start-up events. That probably was the starting point. Maybe it started with the charm of Neil coupled with his intellect and overall persona. Women in their prime and at that level would love to swoon over such guys.

They don't know what they want, but once they are bitten by the charm and intellect, and driven by the fundamentals of beauty and the beast, anything can happen.

To overcome the complexities of her expectations, Rachel decided to keep it simple. She confided in Neil soon. She told him that she wanted to possess him in her heart and that she wanted a lot of attention from him. She did not ask it plainly. There was the entire plan behind this 'to be created scene and set'. That was Rachel's approach all the time. She always wanted to make sure that whatever she did was the best. So she had booked the best suite in Leela Kempinsky at Goa. This was the very next day after the event.

She figured that Neil would be spending time with his business counterparts the next day. She invited Neil for a lunch meeting at the suite. Neil was reluctant at first, however her bio could not be ignored. Rachel was a hundred times richer and more powerful then. She was someone that everyone would vie to spend time with. She wanted to spend time with the guy who she believed would go a long way.

"Neil, I do not have words to express my fondness for you. I am also obliged and grateful that you came to my personal suite at my beck and call," said Rachel as she could not hold on to her happiness on seeing Neil in her complete privacy.

"Hello Rachel! I thought—" Neil said humbly, but he was interrupted by Rachel.

She came closer to Neil and hugged him with a peck on his cheeks. He was taken aback, not because of the hug and the kiss, but it reminded him of what had happened about a couple of years ago. It was like a flashback of what had happened with Drishti. She had approached Neil similarly. He did not necessarily need to equate the two, however that is how he felt at the moment.

So he cautiously pulled back, but not wanting to leave any uneasiness in Rachel, he kissed her back. That was courtesy. But to Rachel, that was having Neil bend the way she had wanted. Like she wanted everyone who she fancied to do so. There was a huge disconnect between the perceptions of the two.

"Thanks, Neil. You have been a wonderful guest."

Contrary to how it was when she had met Neil earlier, now at Madison Square, once she got back after popping some valium, there was nothing wonderful about the guest anymore. That is how it clearly appeared and was evident.

The media was busy clicking photographs and swinging the cameras. They were assigned the targeted jobs. Nobody knew the kind of story that would be published the next day. Even the photographers did not. The more striking and story-laced photographs, better their pay cheques and promotions and incentives. So the stories had a potential to go from just business to personal, crazy insights into the lifestyle of the rich and famous. Nothing would be limited or spared. The desk editors would be tempted into writing it like they would get an orgasm with each click of their keys. They were vultures who would feed on the lives and their consumers would look forward to these feeds. The small bites for the news press were collected from the big wigs.

Rachel found a way to re-approach Neil. She spotted one of the old merchants in the star-studded lobby. So she held the hands of this known guy and walked with him towards Neil. It was not too difficult for her to get Neil out of the sight of Ambani and a few more who had been deeply engaged in business.

"Come on Neil, you've got to meet Captain Majid. You remember your South African deal with Millers?" Rachel said. This was the deal that Neil had worked on, but the way Rachel mentioned it made it clear that it was not her intention to strike off any business discussion.

"Of course I do," said Neil, wondering why she was introducing him.

"Captain Majid has a strong hold in the region, though it is more to do with real estate and mining, and when you needed the raw material—" Before Majid or Neil could react, there was a guest who pulled Majid away in rough haste. It was pre-planned by Rachel. She got Neil back in her 'not so friendly' company.

"Neil, I am warning you one last time, if you don't fuck me tonight, I shall reveal all the dirty secrets that you and I have together and what you did to me. You know the press published only half the story; I shall complete it now."

"Well, there was a story out there, but you bloody got the intern killed. Why did you get him killed? Because the story didn't go the way you had wanted. It was all given a social high profile glam image and you wanted it to be Neil falling over or tripping over Rachel kind of story... darn! You got that boy killed. Obnoxious! How low can you stoop, Rachel? You know I am a dignified man and hence I remained quiet."

"Neil, one last time I tell ya, I shall open my mouth. There is enough paparazzi today that can get your stocks tumbling down with the headlines that I shall provide the juice for."

Rachel's eyes were venomous and it seemed she would certainly sting him tonight. There was apparently no way for him to escape.

Neil was adamant and firm in his approach. He did not budge. And he did that with professional precision, leaving no hint or doubt for the tongue-wagging media.

Rachel kind of evaporated. She was not to be seen after that rejection. It was humiliating for her.

Present day

The village that was about three hundred feet below the hillside that connected Old Havana and Varadero was waiting a few tough cops. This place was about thirty odd miles from the stadium where the music concert was held. The fleet was unexpectedly large. The cops suspected the old Santiago gang which apparently had been dormant ever since Carlos took over the city. Further, when the city was on the transformational path of becoming hi-tech, the gang could barely operate. Any medium they would use to communicate was tracked and crime was no more the viable profession for them. The heist at the museum that helped Carlos go digital was the mastermind of Santiago. He served a few months behind bars and then was released at the behest of the law minister. It was not clear what was the reason, however it was assumed that Santiago's loyalty for communism and the continued reign of communist parties ensured him a free passage. He was released on one condition, rather a promise – he'd not be involved in any crime that would put the image of the country and tourism at risk.

He had agreed and made that unconditional promise to the lawmakers to not operate as a gang leader anymore. Santiago belonged to this village that had now invited the cops, and the reason was Andres.

There was no such address in the village that was given by Andres in the file of Sreedhar's shop. And the only clue that the luxury watch had created was now almost going into the drain. But there was no way on earth that Carlos could let it go. He immediately called up Santiago out of frustration. They spoke in detail.

"*Cómo estás*, Carlos?" (How are you, Carlos?)

"Santiago, *quiero tu ayuda.*" (Santiago, I need your help.)

"*Soy un hombre limpio ahora,*" said Santiago. (I am a clean man now.)

Carlos told him that he needed his help as someone in the mafia or possibly drug cartel had killed a rich billionaire from India. Santiago told him that he was aware of it as it was all in the news. He was very anxious to find out who the perpetrators were as well, for there was the million dollar reward which was very luring. Also, in reality, Santiago's resort business was not fetching him so much money that he was making earlier as a leader of the drug cartel.

"*Santiago, Espero que no estés involucrado en esto en absoluto.*" (Hope you are not at all involved in this crime.)

Santiago told Carlos that he now ran a resort for white people and there was plenty of money in the business. He did not need to kill tourists for money. At the same time, he told Carlos that he was also shocked that a new gang was thriving in the city, and that someone could do this under his nose. Old Havana and the stretch up to 250 miles were all under his control. He activated his network.

He promised Carlos that in the next four hours, he'd give him a tip to take it forward. Carlos knew that Santiago only worked for money, so he offered him money for his help, which was happily accepted. The money was offered for assistance and not necessarily finding the culprits. Carlos told Santiago that he was under tremendous stress to nab the criminals. Santiago asked him if it would be fine to frame anyone at this point to save his ass. Carlos rejected it, stating that the case had international bearing and therefore he had to back the theory with many proofs. Then he murmured something and hung up.

Santiago called all his folks. He was so quick that based on his conversation with Carlos followed by a conversation with a couple of folks, he was able to draw out the entire sketch of what could have possibly happened. There was a time when he was on the other side and hence that knowledge came in handy.

He said to himself, "*Si la tecnología pudiera resolverlo todo, el centro de comercio mundial aún estaría allí en América.*" (If technology could solve everything, the World Trade Center would still be there in America.)

In an hour, five of his most trusted men met him at Iberostar Parque Central Hotel.

They met in the lobby. Unlike his usual self, Santiago ordered a ham burger and a coke. No alcohol or dope. Not today. He was appearing at his best, or at least trying to be. He was seriously committed to solving this. It started with the thousands of dollars Carlos had offered, however in the eyes of people, it was becoming a matter of pride for him. How could anyone dare to commit a crime in his city. That thought pricked all the six of them now. Was it just about pride or anything that might have been inert so far.

Santiago preferred to talk in his broken English at the hotel. He wanted to be seen as a global citizen by the tourists. However, considering the discussion points, he kept a hush tone, in English only though.

"Instead of looking for these two folks, the cops should have put out an advertisement for Andres. I find no reason why he would not have killed them for money. And that is how he got the most expensive watch to sell. It is clear."

Santiago described everything in full detail.

"Agree with you, boss," said Ramos.

Santiago pulled out the photograph and upon seeing it, Ramos reacted sharply.

"This is Andres. He lives in Baracoa. His father works in a chocolate factory," said Ramos.

Santiago knew there was no point discussing anything right now with Ramos. That would be a waste of time. He immediately took out his jeep. Three of his men sat with him and the other two went on to find Andres in case he was around. On the way, Santiago asked Ramos if they should go all the way to Baracoa or ask someone to do the work for them. Time was running out and it was decided they would track Andres rather than go to the place themselves.

"See, I know I am getting greedy here, but I have to think of the foreign couple. If I think of myself and you, then I want to solve it on our own and get the prize money. But if we really need to think of the wellness of the missing duo, then let us tell the cops right now. The unit in Baracoa will trace him and that would be relatively easier. In the interim, we'll look for him in Havana."

"You know boss, what my gut says?"

"Yes, that he is in Havana? Since he has got the money, why would he go back to his village now? Am I correct?"

"You are absolutely correct and…"

"Tell me how do you know Andres? He is no gangsta, is he?"

"Boss, when we had to cross our trucks via Baracoa about four years ago, one of them had broken down, it was Andres and his friends who helped us. I don't remember him because he helped us, but the fact that he had flicked one of our cocaine packets from the space just above the tyres. I saw him doing that. I offered him a place in our gang then, but he refused telling me that he is only good at stealing things and not working for anyone. That guy left an indelible mark in my head and hence I could never forget him. I know where he lives. He was in touch with me for one year. Later on, we just stopped talking."

Santiago got all the information in ten minutes. All the information that was needed. This was done without any cop's involvement. Such was his network. Andres was at the cafe that was about a mile away from the Hotel at Parque Central.

In just about ten minutes, he was picked by Santiago's men. The police was told not to look for him anymore and Carlos was clearly informed of his whereabouts.

Santiago had a rule in his life. He always adhered to it. His role was over the moment Andres was found. Therefore, he wasn't questioned or grilled. He was told that he would be handed over to the cops because they wanted to ask him some questions. That was all.

Carlos's men arrived and took away Andres. Carlos personally called Santiago to thank him and sought his support in the future.

Santiago was aware that a million bucks were on a ride, but he had something else running on his mind.

"Ramos, I want you to find out who is this mole Andres is working for. My name should not come in between. And I want it in two hours. Let the cops do their bit. I want to know who these assholes are, running a filthy game in my Havana," asserted Santiago.

"Sure boss."

Back then at Madison Square Garden –
Awards ceremony

The evening was about to wrap up. Neil was on a ten-minute call with Gauri and he wanted to speak with Neilakshi thereafter. It was a Sunday, a holiday and Neilakshi would have got up by now.

Neil looked extremely happy after talking to his doting daughter.

There was a sudden turn of events as Rachel appeared and asked for quick media attention. She had her manager arrange for this. Neil and the rest of the guests were all hooked to the sight.

"Ladies and gentlemen and all my friends from the glorious media, I am here like your very own. I know in the past, there were issues like my drug habits, my estranged relationships and the latest being my photographs with Neil that were highlighted by the media. I wish I had done this before. I don't care what you wrote about my substance abuse and my crazy flings and all, but I don't want Neil to be dragged into all this. I love his family. His wife Gauri is my dear friend and she gets hurt when you guys drag him into anything. Neilakshi is the most beautiful thing that has happened to them. And Neil, well... he is a thorough gentleman. I am responsible for all that had happened in this past. I hope and wish the family forgives me."

Then she left without even looking at anyone.

There was enough ammunition now in the hall. Everyone was astonished with the admission. The media chased her till the exit area. For the ones who weren't aware, they had a great glimpse into the lifestyle of the elite. For the ones who were aware, they had a great time. In all likelihood, the gossip in the corridors of their high rise estate towers would overshadow anything else. For now, Neil was left to himself. He had no reaction ready. He looked zapped. He was expecting it otherwise, and he began to think in his head. Somehow he did not want the topic to resurface and that is exactly what had just happened.

"What a bitch you are, Rachel! You said it and yet people are talking about how well I could influence you. Maybe you lied for a business deal. Maybe you lied on purpose. You made it sound like that. Fucking jerk. You are trying your level best to keep the topic alive and active. You don't want anyone, especially Gauri, to be happy. You are so ridiculous," said Neil to himself.

He was bombarded with questions that he handled with composure. He left the venue after meeting everyone.

And he sung to himself something that he wrote on his way back to India and had already texted to Gauri:

Myriad thoughts captivated my senses
Uncertain about my future, yet so distinct
Life turns around for me every now and then
To be in the world so shaky that draws upon my instinct
For once I know how it feels when the world looks at you
For once I know how it is when there is a test of times
And I shall get over this with all the love you have for me
For I know I can cross the million oceans and many streams
of rivers
Just because I know I have all your love for me
And here I am going through the rough tides, but I shall sail
them through
And yes, I will have it all and I know, in life, all you need is
love
I have all because I have you.

Present day

Between the town of Havana and Pinar del Río lies a beautiful town of Artemisa. It was founded in 1818 and named after the Greek god of fertility, Artemis. Artemisa is among the most interesting towns with a population of roughly 160,000. It is an attractive and vibrant town with the quintessential Cuban mix of well-preserved neoclassical style, pastel-painted buildings featuring ornate columns in the Doric and Ionic styles.

The setting of Artemisa is certainly an urban one, but it also provides a rustic taste of Cuban country life, as it is a thoroughfare for farmers on horseback. Historically, Artemisa has been a strong cultural centre, and that tradition continues today. The city is home to one of the province's most active Casas de la Cultura, the state-sponsored facilities for plays, music, and other cultural activities.

Artemisa is home to a number of interesting museums, most of which are dedicated to the twenty-four Moncada attackers (out of a hundred and fifty in all) that came from Artemisa.

It is important to note such detailed facts about the town as at some point, Neil and Gauri wanted to establish an Indian temple of Lord Krishna here. There is a long story to it. In short, Carlos had requested Dhanya if they could help set up a temple as he believed in Lord Krishna a lot and he had read somewhere that god had some big connection with the Caribbean. It wasn't an overnight desire, but he had been reading a lot, and when he visited India, he made it a point to go to Vrindavan and spend a day there. Later, Dhanya asked Neil and Gauri if they would be keen, as somewhere she knew they might be.

The couple had marked it as a mandated next step. They believed in god. Building temples and religious places was one of their key goals in life. And then to take it global was a good starting point. That was that.

Here in this town, near one of the oldest museums, was a lane that led to one of the old bright single floor houses. It blended well with the spirit of the town. Inside the house was an old couple – Valencia and Ricardo. In their late sixties, they were ex-employees of Sreedhar. Ricardo practiced medicine till about couple of years ago. He was also rumoured to have worked in a chocolate factory. They had their ancestral house in the municipality of Baracoa. The same place where Santiago's men met Andres. Well, as a matter of fact, he was their only son.

The couple seemed worn out. They were glued to the television sets and were seemingly nervous.

"Valencia, I believe we should inform the cops."

"Don't forget we have promised her not to do that till Neil feels completely alright," said Valencia

"We have applied the best of medicines on his body and you know that he will be fine, so we can take that chance," said Ricardo.

"And, you know if the cops find out, then they will find every other way not to give us the reward," confronted Valencia.

"Look, Gauri has not seen the television news yet, and she has only been holding on to Neil like a crazy wife. It's time we tell her everything and get this out of our system. So far as the reward money goes, we can ask Gauri how to go about it. The money is big, but we can't betray her."

Ricardo and Valencia reached out to the room where Gauri was sitting beside Neil.

Gauri was giving Neil a mild head massage.

She was in a disheveled state. This was after she was being taken care of by the old couple. It was taking a lot of time for her to accept the present moment. It might take forever. She was a survivor. Neil was still not back to his complete senses.

She was braving it. She would murmur and then go quiet. Her physical strength was taking a lot of time to bounce back. It was rather only diminishing. The cases of near death experiences have been far and few. We have all read or heard about them or seen them in the media, but when we go through it ourselves, we can't fathom what it is like. The whole intensity is like a big explosion or a set of mammoth explosions that engulf you and send you into space. One of the most moving stories was that of the kids that survived the Titanic disaster.

Separated from his wife, Michel Navratil decided to run off with their two and four-year-old sons and take them to America to start a new life. He bought second-class tickets for the Titanic and travelled under the alias Louis M. Hoffman.

After the ship struck the iceberg, Navratil regretted the terrible surprise that awaited their mother. One of his sons, Michael J., remembered his father's final words:

"My child, when your mother comes for you, as she surely will, tell her that I loved her dearly and still do. Tell her I expected her to follow us, so that we might all live happily together in the peace and freedom of the New World."

Because the young boys only spoke French and had travelled under an alias without their mother's knowledge, it took her a month to find them. They waited unclaimed in New York until their mother recognized their picture in the newspaper and hurriedly sailed across the Atlantic to retrieve her sons.

Such stories can move anyone. Gauri and Neil had survived a horrific situation, and Neil was kind of still struggling, yet to come out of it.

Gauri looked at Neil and told him she would cut the cake tonight. It was their anniversary. About fifteen years ago, they had tied the knot on this very day. And what a day they had planned – a book launch and their anniversary and the construction of temple and visiting the places they had visited the last time to revive memories. But here they were. Life changed weirdly and abruptly, silent and vulnerable. Now they had almost lost faith in everything. Gauri in particular. She had never done anyone harm in her life.

"Uncle, they were dressed in Cuban cops' uniform. They were cops, I am certain of that, or at least from the appearance that I remember. There were two cars. They were chasing us. I could see them from the rear view mirror. When one of them put on the siren and kind of asked us to pull over, Neil and I were engrossed in an intense discussion and then….." Gauri had begun to cry profusely. She did not want to say anything with Neil around, so they had moved to a different room.

Ricardo looked at Valencia, "Look, there is no point in informing the cops right now. We don't know who are involved and to what extent."

Even though it was hard to understand why the perpetrators would be in the police uniform except for getting a free easy passage, which was not the crucial point, as they only shot the bullets eventually. Nothing could be ruled out.

Valencia was consoling Gauri while she told her to relax and not talk about it right now. She asked her to change the topic and to only talk about herself and her husband as she was intrigued by the love between the two. The old woman was trying to make Gauri think of the strong memories from their past, to give her strength and will. Gauri would always be indebted to this elderly couple. When Valencia asked her to talk about her life, she happily transcended herself into the past.

Life and times of the couple
Five years ago
Upscale Gurgaon, DLF Phase 4

Gurgaon is the satellite city of Delhi and is the leading financial and industrial hub of India. It has architecturally noteworthy buildings in a wide range of styles and from distinct time periods. Gurgaon's skyline with its many skyscrapers is nationally recognized, and the city has been home to several tall buildings with modern planning.

One of the phases in Gurgaon named DLF 4 is amongst the most plush and upscale localities. Neil and Gauri lived on the twenty-third floor. Gauri had started her dental hospital which was a newly-acquired space for her. Bigger and better. Neil was planning to launch his startup, but had no clue yet as to what and how. After whatever the couple had gone through in recent times, they realized who were their friends and who not. They just realized it, but did not know what the formula of identifying such people was.

Well, not just for them, it holds true for anyone. Every relationship and every counsellor preaches it. The foundation of any relationship is trust. Everything else is built on it. The irony is, we begin to trust and then when something goes wrong, the trust is the first thing that goes for a toss. It just shakes everything and you are left wondering, what the fuck just happened. You can fake love, but come to think of it, you can't fake trust. It kills you from inside.

Life will continue to make you meet people like Jerry and Srinya. Betrayals won't stop. Love will come and go. People will come and go. But the ones who stay should be the real genuine ones that you could trust like your very own.

When Jerry deceived Neil, he was definitely hurt as it was a long friendship that died a bitter end. Jerry was extremely close to Neil, but he got greedy and that lured him into something that one would never expect from a true friend. When Srinya deceived Neil, he was hurt as it was a new forming friendship that ended bitterly. Srinya was one person who Neil had always supported in the hardest of times. When people deceive you, it is understood that now you will be cautious in life. However, in reality, it is different. Because not every person is Jerry or Srinya. Not every person will hurt you and cheat you. And definitely, you don't have asshole written on your forehead. Sometimes too much goodness implies that it is actually written on your forehead. That is possible too.

Neil was a good guy. Overloaded with goodness actually. His wife Gauri was still the one who would play safe. She always used to despise Srinya and warned Neil against her. It is a different matter that she warned him because she felt Srinya was coming too close to her hubby. However, when Srinya cheated morally and ethically, Gauri told him, "Neil, you must always listen to your wife. Always."

"Yes Gauri. I do. And I know I fucked up, but now I don't trust people easily. You know trust is the foundation," Neil completed reluctantly.

"Haha, you are such a darling, my baby," said Gauri as she looked at Neil with complete charm.

"You are my baby..." Neil looked back in her eyes.

Neil came closer to Gauri. She held his hands, and repeated what she said a couple of weeks ago when they had gone to one of the stores in the DLF Promenade mall.

"I know I am your baby, but I really want to give you a baby. Look, I am thirty-one now, and you are thirty-five. It's time we seriously plan a child. I don't want our child to think we are goddamn grandparents!"

"Haha, don't worry. We aren't that old yet. How about we have twins?"

"Why can't I be Farah Khan?"

"Would love to have three."

"Neil, suddenly from no plan to have a kid to having three now? Are you alright?"

"Yes, it is the first time you are really talking about it with all seriousness."

"Yes, mom also talked and discussed this with me."

There was a certain serenity in the atmosphere. The couple hugged and slept in each other's arms after a long tiring Friday. Tom's marriage had been fixed with Mehr and there was a lot of running around for them to do.

❖

It was a lovely Saturday morning. Around 6.45 a.m. the sun decided not to show up in this city. Mostly Gauri would wake up in the morning and draw the curtains aside. And the sun would directly fall inside their room, giving the feeling of a pleasant start. Mostly we associate the sunshine with a positive feeling, especially in the colder months. The setting kind of fit perfectly as it was the middle of November.

Mornings are the best time for love. Or so they say. And so did the couple feel. Like always. Neil half-opened his eyes and was certain that the sun wouldn't wake him up as there were dark clouds. The sun wouldn't come out, but the feelings were bright.

Gauri came back and held him around his arms. He sneaked his hand beneath the pillow to find the remote of his Bose system. He had smartly kept the songs in the playlist ready. The morning can be brighter, without the sun too. Everything is possible in love. Possibly brighter and better.

My castle crumbled overnight
I brought a knife to a gunfight
They took the crown, but it's alright
All the liars are calling me one
Nobody's heard from me for months
I'm doing better than I ever was, 'cause
My baby's fit like a daydream
Walking with his head down
I'm the one he's walking to
So call it what you want, yeah, call it what you want to
My baby's fly like a jet stream
High above the whole scene

Loves me like I'm brand new
So call it what you want, yeah, call it what you want to
All my flowers grew back as thorns
Windows boarded up after the storm
He built a fire just to keep me warm
All the drama queens taking swings
All the jokers dressin' up as kings
They fade to nothing when I look at him
And I know I make the same mistakes every time
Bridges burn, I never learn, at least I did one thing right
I did one thing right
I'm laughing with my lover, making forts under covers
Trust him like a brother, yeah, you know I did one thing right
Starry eyes sparkin' up my darkest night
My baby's fit like a daydream…
So call it what you want, yeah, call it what you want to
I want to wear his initial
On a chain round my neck
Not because he owns me
But 'cause he really knows me
Which is more than they can say,
I recall late November, holdin' my breath
Slowly I said, "You don't need to save me
But would you run away with me?"
Yes (would you run away?)
My baby's fit like a daydream
Walking with his head down
I'm the one he's walking to

…

Tailor Swift kept playing on loop. Love was in the air. They could feel it in their embrace. This kept them young and going. And the morning love. Wow.

Gauri looked into his eyes and said drawing him closer, "I love you as I always did, and I must tell you one more thing today. I want twins. Please give me twins."

Neil smiled and began to kiss her lips gently. Like he was half asleep but feeling it completely. That fresh kiss in the morning did all the magic. Gauri went deeper in his mouth and took out the pillow from below his head and moved it aside. She was atop, and the kiss lasted forever. The foreplay lasted way longer than they could imagine. They made love. It was sensual and mesmerizing. Like both were completely lost in each other.

"How beautiful it is to begin a day like this? How beautiful it is to be loved by the one you can't live without," said Gauri.

"How beautiful it is to love the one you can't live without," exhaled Neil.

Neil was moving his fingers over Gauri's nude back and she was entangled between his legs from her waist. They were feeling each other as they chatted. The breeze blew into the room gently, caressing Gauri's hair.

"Let's think of four names to complete the combination of our twins," said Neil.

"Neilakshi, Neilesh, Mehr and Brahma. What say?" replied Gauri.

"That was really quick, Gauri." Neil looked at her with surprise.

"I was ready with them ever since I spoke with mom."

"Mehr? Tom would be very happy. But then it will be a whole lot confusing, won't it?" asked Neil.

"I love that girl, you know. I am so happy they are getting married. The same name for our kid was more out of the emotions that I carry for her."

The chatting continued. The love continued, it never stopped anyway. The preparations continued.

"Listen, Neil. Let's do it one more time. I read somewhere, the probability of a pregnancy increases with more times the intercourse."

"And don't tell me you read all this after talking to mom, and hence you want to follow a prescribed love diet now," chuckled Neil.

"A woman is ready with her body and plans when she wants to take that leap. So yes, I have done all my homework. Don't forget that I am a doctor. Let's follow the prescription."

"*Daanto ki* doctor…" giggled Neil.

"Huh. So what? Still a doctor na."

"Come on now, or you will keep wasting time showing off, honey."

Neil grabbed Gauri slowly by her shoulders and kept pulling her towards his chest. Her breasts lay comfortably on his body as he held her face towards his. Up and close. He moved his fingers on her lower lip. And kissed it slowly.

"You know Neil, I can't believe that even after so many years of our marriage, we make love like we are in our twenties… with so much passion. Knock on the wood."

"Yes honey. And you know, you are still as beautiful as you were the first time I met you," Neil said while kissing her neck.

"Neil, if I weren't beautiful or hadn't been like this, would you have stopped loving me?"

"And I know what you want to hear and you know what my answer will be, don't you?"

"Still, say it na. I love to hear it from you. Your words and your feelings melt me."

"I believe it's our love that makes you and me beautiful."

"Fuck! How do you weave such words?"

"And you thought only you are spontaneous, dentist... I mean, doctor."

"You are such a...." Gauri slowly bit Neil's ear. And swirled her tongue inside. They stopped talking. Neil was completely aroused and Gauri was all excited. She kissed his chest and slowly went down kissing. They made out passionately yet again. The music made it heavenly and the wind was a catalyst. Both slept naked, holding on to each other, their bodies and souls entwined.

It was 4 p.m. Mild showers and cool temperature brought cheer to the residents of this suburb. However, this did not hold true for everyone. Tom was quite nervous and the weather did no good to him. His wedding was only a few days away. And Neil wasn't picking up the phone. On the other hand, Mehr had been trying to reach Gauri, and she wasn't responding either. His bestie was not around and he wanted him like 24/7. He knew his experienced buddy would come in handy even more than his parents. Though his entire clan had gathered, inside his heart, there were thoughts that he could only share with Neil. Something like, 'Dude what should my preparations for the first night be?' In other words, for his *suhaag raat*. Was there any way on this planet to ask your normal set of friends this? No way. Parents were a definite no. Even though Indian parents try their best that their kids ask them everything. But they forget that when the kids from 80s were growing up, as soon as Pooja Bedi would appear on TV in the *Kamasutra* condoms ad, it would be them who would switch channels or leave the room.

Finally, after an impatiently long wait, Neil called Tom back.

"*Abbey saaley kahan hai? Holiday wala* had come from Thomas King. And I couldn't finalize the place without talking to you. And we need to close down on this online shopping list. Mom is asking me what I want so she can gift us, so I told her that I shall check with you. *Tu kya laa raha hai?*"

"What the fuck, Tom? Hahahahaha… A*a rahe hain hum* in an hour or so."

Neil looked around. Gauri had hit the shower. He knocked at the door seeking permission to go inside.

"Neil, are you sure you aren't on viagra?" She laughed and half opened the door. Her body was covered with foam and water drops rolled down her face and hair, making her sexier.

"Babes, I just wanted to get my trimmer. I had left it in here, and by the way, you are my natural Viagra, so why would I need any from outside."

Neil put half his head and face between the door and stretched his hands to the trimmer while Gauri picked it and handed it over to him. He looked at his wife, teasing her, wiping off the foam from her skin and said, "If only we did not have to go to Tom's right now, I would have shown what kind of potion you are to me," he said as he closed the door.

Little could he focus then, as his phone was abuzz with frantic calls from the would-be anxious groom. Gauri also hurriedly came out.

Just when they were about to stagger out, Gauri got Neil his watch that he had forgotten, "Here you go. I hope I can buy you your favourite Omega watch soon."

Present day

"Aunt Valencia, it is our wedding anniversary today and I am going to bake a cake. I want to do it on my own. A chocolate marble cake is what Neil loves the most."

Valencia could see the love in the eyes of the lady.

"You know, I have been telling Andres to find a girl for himself and get married soon. He needs to bring us a cheer and find a girl like you. And then she will bake a cake for us," she chirped.

Gauri reached out to Valencia and hugging her from behind, asked," Auntie, where is the baking soda kept?"

Beaming with natural joy arising out of compassion, Valencia placed everything that was needed in order. Gauri then asked for a phone reluctantly, "I don't know where ours disappeared after the accident, but Auntie, I shall just use yours for a quick call to India, if you permit?"

Valencia obliged with a 'do not even ask' look.

Gauri took the phone, and kept biting its top corner in nervousness. Almost twenty-four hours of this ordeal had passed. While she knew her world would have gotten disturbed on the other side of the globe, she kept away from any sort of communication on purpose. That would have meant a lot of explaining, talking, and discussing. But all she wanted to do was be by her husband's side and that was it. She wanted nothing at all. Plus, she wanted to be completely safe and secure. The feeling was different from what one would imagine.

You survive a disaster. Come back alive from the clutches of death. For many moments, you aren't able to believe that you're actually alive. The feeling is like you have reached higher and higher up in the skies. Then it takes a hell lot of effort and time and love from your people to let the feeling sink in. There is a simple trajectory. From the state of near death to shock, disbelief, to realization, and then to normalcy. And this doesn't happen in merely twenty-four hours. And that's precisely why Gauri was quiet initially. It was only now that she attempted to open her mouth. Her condition was more precarious. Neil had not come to his complete senses as yet.

> *The sound of the crash still haunts me*
> *I find my pillows wet each morning*
> *The dream which leaves me with raining tears*
> *The reality of life each one fears.*
>
> *I want you with me each moment,*
> *I want you to embrace me now;*
> *Why are you still sleeping, my heart questions you;*
> *Why do you need a machine to breathe instead of me, it's crying;*

The files you left before leaving
Remind me of how careless you've been;
You came in to see me in such a rush
And have left my world now in utter hush;

With the kiss I parted;
If only I was persistent about your safety
Like I protected my love for you;
I would have had you around me now
Jumping and dancing…

I have two pieces of paper with me,
One with future of graphs and numbers
The other with your heart beat range;
I'm tearing the former and sitting next to you now,
Why don't you wake up and smile at me?

"Gauri, I wanted to tell you that we've had three doctor visits already for Neil while you were asleep. We did not want to tell you, and just pretended that Ricardo is curing your husband. He practiced medicine only briefly and we did not want to take a chance with your husband. But I thought I should tell you now. The main doctor will be here any moment. And do not worry, he is like our family."

Gauri had tears rolling down her cheeks. She kept the phone aside. Her hands were slightly powdered with cake dough. She rolled her sleeves, exhaled a few times, and then wiped her face with her curled up fist. As a predictable reaction, rested both her hands on Valencia's shoulders.

"In this country, where on the one hand, we have been attacked in such a brutal inhuman manner, on the other we have you, who are so selfless and so damn caring when they don't need to. Auntie, when you tell me all this, I only feel heavily loaded in my chest. I would never be able to repay what you have done for us. If ever needed – my blood, my soul, my life – whatever can ever aid you in your life, is yours. And I know you won't accept it, yet let me say this, so I feel a bit lighter. Please Auntie, I am so shattered… I am so overwhelmed…"

Gauri sobbed violently and held Valencia in her arms. Valencia also could not stop herself. She broke down completely.

This is what it is about human emotions. You don't let them pent up. You let them out. Often. As and when. Like it was the mental and emotional state right now.

"Gauri, I don't have a daughter. All I want from you is to love me like a daughter would. That's all I want from you, my child. And do not worry, your love will heal Neil. No doctor is needed. I see that. I can see the improvement in him. You are such a loyal and doting wife. Your life reminds me of mine. Listen, you call up your folks now. They must be so worried."

"Yes Auntie. I was waiting for the right time. Let me do that now."

Gauri moved to the terrace. She decided to call up at Mehr's. She inhaled deeply and kind of prepared herself to talk. Her hands were trembling. She had just come out of an emotionally heavy discussion with Valencia and was now diving into another. All of this and the life-altering event that she had faced… it was natural to feel this way.

It was 7 a.m. in India. Mehr had slept late after speaking with the cops, relatives and everyone else who could possibly help.

The phone rang and disconnected on its own. Gauri tried again and wasn't able to reach her number. She tried calling Tom instead. His number was not reachable too.

"Damn it guys! Your network sucks when needed the most. I would only advise everyone to always have an alternate connection. Gosh, what am I thinking right now. Think of a solution Gauri, a solution… hmm. God help me. I can't think. I need to talk to Mehr. Hmm… let me send a message to her on Instagram and Facebook. *Saala wifi toh chal raha hoga!*" She was furiously frustrated.

She logged into her Facebook, and immediately sent a message to the couple together. And then with some hope, she came downstairs. For one thing was very clear in her head. She would not converse with anyone at this point. Not her parents, not Neil's, nor anyone else. Only Tom or Mehr. That's where there journey to Cuba had started from. She wanted solutions and a plan for the way ahead. She remembered a few classy lines that her favourite author had written:

It is not the worries that bring you down
It is not the sorrows that pull you around
It is the fear of unknown that creates havoc
It is the pain of past that shrouds your senses
The Almighty sends the powers to awaken it
He sends you the magic that you can't fathom
He alleviates your fears and instills it all

Take his name and go back to your world
Wait for the powers to heal to fulfill
Your dreams and desires and all that you need
Go back to your world let him act
Go back…

In the main city of La Habana, Santiago was pretty active with his key folks. After handing over Andres to the cops, he decided to take Ramos and a couple of other folks along to the accident site. He wanted to play a bigger role in solving the crime. His close association with the communist party was instigating him deep inside. The weather was humid. He picked his favourite corona on the way.

Ramos drove an old Ford Mustang. It was Santiago's all time favourite. It kept him grounded and reminded him of his not so glorious days. This was brought from a drug dealer then as a bargain to help him solve his brother's murder case. That was about a decade-and-a-half ago. He had ever since carried the reputation of finding moles in the network. Even though he left the crime scene, he was still the favourite of Carlos in many aspects. And now he was heavily depending on him.

Carlos called him up, "San, listen, this boy Andres is not opening his mouth. I don't wanna kill him. Look man, I am handing him back to you. I know you had said you will solve it all for me in two hours. An hour's already gone. I have to make a press announcement, man, and I am in deep trouble. The government is putting a lot of pressure on me. Their PM and external affairs minister are chasing ours. It's a real big one. I feel so stupid that I am not able to find two people in my own city. Help me. Find those Indians soon."

"Okay, look I am going to the spot, chief. You can hand over that boy to Junior. He shall be at your station in ten. Now let me do my work. But you make me one promise."

"The million dollars will be yours, San…" Carlos said. He was sounding a lot perturbed today. Maybe it was more than the political pressure.

"I don't want that money. You take it or distribute to the poor. I want you to help me win the elections… I think it is best to be a politician."

The top cop showed his weakness to ex drug dealer and the latter asked him to help him win the elections. Such is the cycle of power. For once, Santiago did wonder as to why would Carlos hand it over to him so confidently. The thought did not stay in his head for long as he was assigned a task that he was himself keen in closing.

Ramos reached the point and parked the car right at the edge that was about four feet away from the tree that was hit by the victims' car. Santiago sat inside for a few minutes while carefully inspecting the surroundings with his observant eyes. Ramos stood at the edge of the cliff, looking down the trench, wondering what could've possibly gone wrong the day before. Within five minutes, Santiago stepped out with both his men and continued to be carefully silent. He was not supposed to be disturbed. He carried his pair of binoculars, a notepad, pen, camera and some dry fruits in his shoulder bag. In his right hand he continued to sip his corona. Santiago crossed to the other side of the street.

He kept walking while removing a pile of papers, polythene, pebbles before hitting into shards of glasses and some remnants of painted iron boards. He stopped and lifted a portion of a broken rectangular board.

"Hey Ramos, come here quick!"

Ramos almost flew to his boss. Santiago instructed him to search the area meticulously and find him all the other broken parts of the piece of metal. While Ramos continued his job at his boss's behest, Santiago crossed back to the site of the accident. After ten minutes, he called up Carlos and sought his time for an urgent meeting. Carlos arrived within five minutes as he was close by. He started revealing what could have possibly happened.

"Carlos, you would have already done your investigation and therefore whatever I suggest could be a possible match or a mismatch. However, feel free to ask. As far as I am concerned, you are very close to solving the case. But I am still wondering and confused as to why this place was not scanned properly. Anyway, your men must be lazy."

Carlos felt confident about Santiago's claim. Also, he heard the last part of Santiago's words and kind of went uneasy.

"This was a preplanned murder. It was carefully planned, but was supposed to be done differently. The criminals, I mean the perpetrators, chased the car and wanted to kill them when they would move out of the car near the village as they were planning to go there to attend the food festival.

"There were two cars that were chasing them. Both the cars had identical number plates. They were supposed to be joined by someone else, and at this point, I don't know who. The license plate had the name 'iSABellA'. Both of them in the same font and pattern. After the chase, they were about to shoot them as they saw the couple had rolled down the window, but there was another car coming from the front, so they missed it. The couple did not notice they were being chased. However, it could not be completely ruled out as the accident could the due to the fact that they began to speed as they realized they were being chased, or the driver lost control... maybe due to an argument or lack of sleep. Right now, anything is possible, but I shall be certain about it soon."

Carlos couldn't believe it for a second and without wasting much time, told him that he was correct so far and that he would be interested in knowing how he arrived at such a precise conclusion at a later point in time. For now, he wanted Andres to open up and talk about how he landed up with Neil's watch.

Santiago laughed and gave sarcastic hints to Carlos. "Ever since the cartel has softened and the mafia has died down, and people like us have got into ethical businesses, it looks like the police have lost the magic of straightening out criminals."

Santiago reached out to Carlos and whispered in his ears, "Look boss, I know you very well. You are either hiding something or up to something. If you don't want to tell, that is fine."

Carlos stiffened himself, coughed a little and said in a low tone, but kept it harsh.

"No, that's not the thing. This case has a lot of limelight and if I end up beating this prick and he dies, then I will be in trouble. I tried every other way, but he won't say a word."

"Andres, look, if you tell me the truth, then we will find these people and you will get a portion of the money," said Santiago.

"Okay, I will tell you everything, but you promise that you won't say anything to my parents."

"Yes, don't worry. Can you now open your mouth? We are running out of time," Santiago said sternly.

"Okay, I saw the watch in my parents' room. I knew this was an expensive watch. I thought my parents got it from somewhere and they did not know it's worth. I could not ask them and stole it. That's all. I sold it. Please do not drag my old parents into it."

"How old are they?"

"Around sixty-five," Andres said nervously.

"Then I doubt they are running a crime or smuggling racket here. Your old parents are in for big trouble. The man who owns this watch is a billionaire from India and has been murdered. Your parents have a lot of questions to answer," said Santiago.

The phone rang. Valencia handed it over to Gauri immediately.

She grabbed it with trembling hands.

"Mehr… Mehr… uhhh…"

She cried unstoppably, and Mehr did the same. They could not talk to each other at all for the first few minutes.

"Gauri… Gauri… are you safe? Say yes or no?"

"Yes…," she said with her teeth chattering as she leaned on the wall for support.

Suddenly she realized that she needed to be with Neil while she was talking. She returned to the room in a rush and sat beside him. She held his fingers, moved hers between his and kept talking to Mehr.

"Oh my god! We were so worried. Like not able to sleep at all. You both have been constantly on our minds and we had no clue what to do. I just want to know everything," Mehr moved to the other room as she did not want Neilakshi to wake up.

Gauri gave her all the details. She mentioned how she was avoiding calling in the last few hours and how the cops over here couldn't be trusted much. While the cops' uniform of the murderers was on her mind, also the fact that the cops were not able to nab the criminals in the last twenty-four hours, left a negative impact on her. She narrated everything and told her to keep Dhanya informed.

"Listen, do tell Dhanya a few things so that she is aware. I know she has some cop links in Cuba, but tell her to avoid telling them anything till she is certain of who is involved. This is the number that I can be reached at," Gauri spoke quickly.

"Gauri, don't rush, please. I want to know everything in detail. And listen, we are reaching there tomorrow. Can we come to stay with you? Look, have you informed Alicia yet? And listen, one more thing, we are there for you, okay? How sweet of the couple that took care of you," said Mehr in a single breath.

"Yes, I really want you guys to come tomorrow. How's my Neilakshi doing? No, I have not informed Alicia yet. I shall do now. *Neilakshi kaisi hai, bol na?*"

"She is fine. She is not aware of anything. We've managed to keep her away. We have told her you are travelling and hence your network is not reachable."

"Send me her pics on this phone."

"Yes, will do. Gauri, you have no idea what I am feeling right now. *Humari phat gayi thi yaar*. No more Cuba for you guys. And yes, we will nail the criminals. You know the PM assured the nation that this will be solved within twenty-four hours."

"What the fuck are you saying? It's not actually even twenty-four hours and the Prime Minister has addressed the nation? Wondering why Valencia has kept me away from watching the television."

"There's a two-million award for you guys. It was a million and now it is doubled. And it is only applicable when you are found alive. So that was some respite."

"Really! Wow. That's awesome. We are so important to the world? And you guys are such a support. And do let Dhanya also know. Don't forget. And send pics. Don't forget that also. Rest later. Love you darling."

"Okay, you too take care, and don't worry, Neil will be fine. We are coming with Dr Komalbir. Remember he is the number one in India when it comes to cases like these. And you must get him admitted to a hospital asap. Don't worry, the cops will protect you."

"Okay, bye now."

Gauri felt relieved and more comfortable. Till such a time you get around the people that belong to you, there will be a normal natural strangeness. Even though Gauri was more concerned about her husband and their overall safety, and Valencia and Ricardo had helped them heal, yet it was after talking to Mehr and finding out that her daughter was fine and hearing the words of comfort from her, that she felt nearly fine.

She had a smile on her face and gratitude in her heart. She

handed the phone back to Valencia who refused to take it from her. She was very clear. She told her to keep it with her. The phone would be her mode of communication with her people.

Suddenly the phone rang and Gauri picked it up instinctively. The voice from the other side was that of a guy who said, "Mommy, where are you? Please tell me. The cops are looking for you. I am sorry, mommy, I stole the watch today. It belonged to some foreigners who are missing. They feel I have done something to them. And they also feel you are involved in all this. You have to meet them otherwise they will beat me black and blue. Mommy, you there?"

Gauri disconnected the phone. She took a deep breath and looked at the phone while tapping her feet heavily on the floor. Then she reached out to Valencia.

"Auntie, your son Andres took Neil's watch and sold it. That led the cops to him. Now the cops are coming for you. I don't want any trouble for you or him. Which means they can be here any moment," gasped Gauri.

"Andres stole the watch? I can't believe he has not left all this. He has got into trouble in the past for petty crimes. Will he ever turn a new leaf?"

Valencia felt horribly guilty. She did not even react to the other part about the cops and was stuck at her son being a thief. Gauri made an effort to help her snap out of it as she said, "Auntie, that is not the point. The cops are coming for you and they will be here any moment. So let's call them before they find us and cause you any trouble."

"But they don't know where we are. And you relax. We won't do anything till you are sure."

"Auntie, please call up the police right now. Please also call up the media. I just want the two million dollars to be yours officially. Else it will go to the cops. And I don't want that to happen."

❖

About twenty-two kilometres east off Havana is the suburb of Alamar, also named Alamar-Playa, part of the municipio of Habana del Este. This district is primarily a prefabrication construction of Soviet-style architecture. Because of this, Cuban poet Juan Carlos Flores has described it as 'The Heart of the Russian Barrio'.

At one point in time, the town had an active mafia. There were multiple gangsters. Their areas were divided well. That was the past. Things had changed now.

It was 5 p.m. Havana time. About a kilometre east off the Main Avenue was hotel Espana. On the fifteenth floor, in room 1501, there was some unusual activity going on. The room was equipped with satellite phones, monitors that were connected to CCTVs. A man in a husky Spanish tone was talking in broken English. It seemed he was on an international call.

"Hola! Senora! You never told us anything about them. The power they hold. The entire country is looking for them. I need the remaining money transferred asap so that I can fly to Russia. And please add half a million more as the reward money has also gone up to two million dollars. I want my fees to be four-and-a-half million dollars now."

"First thing first, I want you to know that there is no link between what you were assigned and who the victims were. The price of four million USD is worthy of what you deserve. Half a million raise for what? That was not agreed upon. And yes, your remaining two million dollars shall be in your account by tomorrow morning. And also, you are not supposed to call me directly. You know you are only supposed to be dealing with Isabella."

"Well, I hear you. I will deal with Isabella. Just like you, Isabella is also a contact for me who I have never seen or met. And so far as the money goes, I am adamant about the half a million raise as the expenses have gone up in this case. We had to pay huge money to the people who would help the authorities to distract from the case and the evidences. Hope you understand. And Isabella is not the sponsor of this crime, you are. For any commercial discussion, I shall only deal with you. Now stop acting smart and send me the two-and-a-half million dollars by tomorrow."

The phone was disconnected even before the conversation could end.

The doorbell rang. He looked into the peephole. It was his colleague. Another one from the dormant gang.

"Come on in, Carl."

"Thanks Freddie. We are all set to leave the country in two days. Any luck on the bodies of the couple?"

"No no, they must have been eaten by the animals."

"That lady might stop our payment. She's clear that we should have found the bodies by now. We are not even certain if they are actually dead."

"Carl, she did not tell us that the car was bulletproof. That isn't our mistake. She only sent these photographs and that's about it. If she messes with us, you know the cops are going to back us."

"She does not live here, so we would be caught if the issue escalates. She is a Russian and they are bloody powerful here in Cuba. They supply arms and money and lot of products to our country."

"Nope, we won't be caught. When have you seen drug dealers here getting punished! Pablo Escobar and El Chapo were stupid. We are not. We are into clean and ethical business. Killing two foreigners who came to fuck around with us in our own country is not a crime. It is nothing but protecting ourselves. Also, I have one of my men on the job. He used to work for me earlier. I have promised him a position in politics. He runs his resorts. He shall be of great help too."

Freddie seemed way too confident about everything that was there. But Carl was cautious.

Freddie received a call on his phone. He stepped aside and spoke, "Isabella, I just told the Russian lady to send me the rest of the money."

"If you ever say anything to anyone without seeking my permission, your carcass won't be recovered on or inside the earth or the whole of the Caribbean. Do you understand that?"

"Yes, sure I do. I apologize." The line went blank.

"Haaaaaaaaaaaaa!" Freddie screamed. He felt humiliated but he had no option. He knew well that the person who could pay him so much money or threaten him and ran a network like this would be extremely powerful.

❖

It was evening. The weather seemed to be tilting towards rain. Artemisa would soon be a stop point for the cops if the elderly couple revealed it. Even if they didn't, the cops would figure their location using mobile detection as Andres kept this mouth shut. But it was the unprecedented rains that kind of brought the town to a complete halt. There was a landslide on the way as well that cut off the house from the rest of the town. The couple took the decision of moving from the village to this town deliberately.

Gauri sat beside Neil. She wiped his face with the kerchief and used her fingers to wipe away the moisture. Then she held his hand, and kissed him again. She had changed his shirt some time back. It was a new one bought by Ricardo. Gauri prayed silently as she held her husband's hand. Then she smiled at him as she remembered how Neil had wooed her a few days ago with the song sung by Arijit. She searched for it and began playing it on Valencia's cell through YouTube.

Pal... do pal... ki hi kyun hai zindagi
Is pyar ko hai sadiyan kaafi nahin
To khuda se maang loon
Mohlat main ek nayi
Rehna hai bas yahan
Ab door tujh se jana nahin...
Jo tu mera humdard hai
Jo tu mera humdard hai
Suhana har dard hai...
Jo tu mera humdard hai

Music holds immense powers. There is no denying that. And when you love someone so bad, it has the prayers of millions of people. God surely listens to those prayers. As Gauri hummed the song while looking at Neil, the atmosphere changed. True love and concern was palpable in the air. Within a few minutes, Neil moved his toe. Gauri froze in joy, without batting an eyelid. The joy was so intense that the thunderstorms and heavy noise of the downpour did not make any impact. She was completely deafened to all external factors. She forgot where she was and the circumstances she was in. It was all inert. It was meaningless. She knew this was real. For the first time her husband had moved a bit. Was it her love or the music or the natural self or her prayers being answered by god? It was difficult to ascertain that at this point. However, Valencia said something that she would not be able to forget in a long time to come.

"At the crossroads, when god makes a decision of pulling human life away from the treacherous earth and is certain of freeing his or her soul, there is one and only one power and that is the power of the love of a soulmate that can make him alter his decision. And we in Cuba truly believe in it. I am assuring you with utmost certainty that god has given your husband back to you and now it is only going to get better. Celebrate, for he can be touched by no evil. Celebrate this new life. This new breath that you have gained. Just make the best of everything now. Nothing can go wrong."

"Auntie, I know that god has been there, but for me and my husband, it is you. It is you and your husband who god sent. You are the harbinger of god for us. You are a blessed soul. Thanks again, Auntie." Gauri kissed her hand and continued.

"Auntie, I want to know more about you and uncle, please. I am so curious. This part of the world to me was all rum and cigars, and music and fun. When I see you both, I see so much love and discipline. I want to know all about you. I am so curious about your life story."

"Oh! There is a long story that I shall tell you and Neil together, but to cut it short, let me tell you the key elements of our life," Valencia said, smiling like a wise one. The bond between the two was becoming stronger. The ladies were now carefree and seemed to have forgotten the hardships for a moment. This is what enriching company does to you. There is a sense of security and liberation that engulfs you. Also, for an old woman, to have the company of this young woman was most welcoming. Having a young boy who was unemployed and who kept frequenting prison, and a retired husband, Gauri was like a breath of fresh air in her otherwise mundane and robotic life.

"Mind if I get some rum for you? Coconut flavour? I shall mix it with pineapple juice and you shall feel relaxed," said Valencia.

"Hahaha, sure my sweet Auntie. I certainly would, for I have a reason now. I love Malibu back home."

Valencia brought three glasses, two with coconut rum and one dark rum for Ricardo, who was glued to the television set, watching the news. This family did more than one could have expected even from one's own family. No matter what Gauri asked of them, they would do knowing what was best for her and Neil.

"Gauri, we fell in love at Hemingway's library. Actually, he fell in love with me first. He would always borrow the book that I returned at the library. That was cute, you know. So he ended up reading all the books that I had. I could see that from the table I sat at. He would sit diagonally opposite me. I got very curious about him and decided to ask him about his interest in exactly the same books that I borrowed. So I approached him one day. He looked at me as if he had never seen me before. Such a crazy boy he was. The reason he gave me was that it was merely coincidental that he had picked up those books after me. So that was the beginning. And he smartly read the books because when we got further into a conversation, he and I had a lot to talk about. Also, I am impressed with boys and men who like reading. And you will be surprised that he was the only boy in the library. The rest were all girls. I look back now and feel I was lucky. To have a boy fall for me when there were a dozen girls around me was plain lucky. We love each other the same way even now. And you both remind me of my times." Valencia's eyes moistened. It was nostalgic for her. Gauri was completely enamoured by their tale.

Ricardo joined them after finishing his rum. "Valencia, did you tell Gauri about our charm for Lord Krishna and the plans we have for the future?"

"Gauri, we have a fondness for Lord Krishna here. A big trustee is present in La Habana. We have got land allotted here in this city by the minister under Raul Castro. And someone in India seems to be interested in constructing ten temples in the country, with one right here. We are so happy. What we also got to know was that the trust was not very happy that someone in India had got this huge contract of building temples across the country. Anyway that is that. You know we read the *Bhagawad Gita* way back in the library itself. We discovered Lord Krishna then. Ever since, we have loved him."

Ricardo and Valencia shared this love for the god together. He even had an idol of the god in absolutely Indian style. He washed his hands, brushed his teeth and then touched the feet of the idol before getting it out to show them.

"Uncle, I could have visited the temple that you would have set up here. You don't need to put in so much effort," said Gauri.

"Okay, I was told that I cannot put Lord Krishna anywhere just like that. It has to be laid on some auspicious foundation on the right day. So we have just been waiting for the temple to be built here. Only then we will place Lord Krishna over there. For now, I have kept him in the room in one corner that remains undisturbed," Ricardo said looking at Gauri, seeking her approval.

"Okay Uncle. And I shall pray to god that the temples get constructed soon. I am so amazed to learn the amount of sincerity you regard Lord Krishna with."

"Sure, kid. Thank you."

"Ricardo, let me make you another drink. You can put Krishna back. And then I believe Gauri will feed Neil now. I would like to hear from her about her life and all that has happened and the circumstances that led her into this situation."

As Ricardo left, the rains continued and the television ran news headlines of imminent danger that the rains posed. He sipped his rum and waited for the perfect time to inform the government about Gauri and Neil. He had to inform the media as well, taking the clue from Gauri's discussion with his wife. He had not approached the cops as yet deliberately. And so far as his son was concerned, he knew he would be fine. This was not his first visit to prison. He was also upset about the whole episode of him stealing the watch. This couple had built such a strong bond with the young couple. He found Gauri and her husband to be really good people. His son stealing from them, though in ignorance, was not acceptable.

Valencia was all ears. She asked Gauri again about all that had happened from the time of the wedding of Tom and Mehr. Gauri excitedly confirmed that in about forty hours, she would make her meet them, along with Neilakshi.

Tom and Mehr's wedding

The stage was all set for Tom and Mehr's wedding. It was an extravagant night. Neil and Gauri were around the couple for almost a week prior to their wedding. Mehr looked like a doll. She was decked up in Manish Malhotra couture. Her footwear was recently gifted to her by Gauri. Tom was wearing a sherwani by Sabyasachi.

The entire venue gave the feeling of a Spanish garden. It was done in mostly white, that gave an elegant appeal. They had spent a decent amount on the three-day long wedding which was more like a festival.

The next day was the day of the grand reception. It was being held at Leela Kempinsky in Goa. People flew in from Mumbai, Delhi, Kolkata and as far as Dubai and Tashkent, Havana, and Bangkok.

Leela Kempinsky, a plush resort, was a great choice in Goa. Away from the hustle bustle of the main city, in the serene part of southern Goa at Salcete beach, it was set on a 75-acre property with a private beach, lagoons and tropical gardens. Featuring balconies, and tropical or contemporary decor, the rooms that were booked for guests had access to a private pool area.

The property boasted of four restaurants, bars, an outdoor pool, a gym and an Ayurvedic spa, as well as a twelve-hole golf course and tennis courts.

"Bhai, this place is awesome. Thanks for booking it," said Tom to Neil.

Neil and Gauri had made all the arrangements. According to Neil, this was the least he could do for his best pal.

"But bro, where the fuck is James? His number is not reachable."

"He texted me. He is on the way. Guess what? He is coming with his wife. That is brilliant!"

"Yeah, he is coming with his fourth wife. Hope this one stays with him!"

As the evening continued, and the delicacies and cocktails made its way through the guts of the guests, there were some surprises in store that included mind-blowing performances from Neil's favourite stand-up comedian and a fine actor, Zakir Khan. He had been Gauri's favourite actually. Once Gauri had treated his dental problem and had found him to be absolutely grounded and humble. That is when they decided to invite Zakir for the wedding. The actor refused any payment. So did Mika. Neil and Mika's relationship went back a long way, when he and his six brothers, including Daler Mehendi used to perform together. That is when Neil was studying in college. He had invited him then. At that time Mika was less known amongst the masses. Neil invited him a few times and that did get him huge support within the University of Delhi. While his success cannot be simply attributed to people like Neil who gave him huge importance and respect when his career was not going anywhere, yet it was clear in Mika's head that these were the people who were selfless and never chased fame. He was just one call away. Such a super star was Mika. So was Zakir Khan.

Neil and Gauri were put up in the corner quarter that was diagonal to the swimming pool. Neil wanted to change into a new pair of clothes so he decided to check into his room. Gauri mingled with the guests and kept them company.

Neil stretched himself and staggered his way to his temporary dwelling. On his way, as he crossed the pool, he bumped into a tall pretty girl. To Rachel, it was not a mishap, but a happy encounter. Neil said sorry a few times, as if he was at fault, though it was unintentional. He just wanted to change quickly and return to the party. Rachel had a great time at the event, but was looking for some peaceful and quiet corner. She could have spent forever here by the poolside. That is how it appeared.

"Hello, I am Rachel. You might not know me, but Mehr happens to be my old friend from college."

"Hello, I am Neil. Bhargav. I mean Neil Bhargav. I don't know how much you know about me, but I just happen to be the groom's best friend. Like, we have known each other ever since we were kids."

"So that's—" Rachel stopped abruptly and pointed at Neil's face. There was a mosquito.

"Oh thank you. I think I've got to go," said Neil as he realized that he was slightly high and held up with a pretty lass. Any further interaction might lead to chaos.

"Hey listen… I have heard you at a startup event and I was pretty impressed with you. How come you forgot me? You remember at the event at Leela, a woman reached out to you. I am the same woman. Neil, look, I have a business proposition for you."

"Damn yes, I vaguely remember. But you have what… a business proposition?" Neil asked with much emphasis. He was thoroughly confused.

"I have a business proposition…."

"Yeah, I heard that. I mean, what and why, and do you even know me except for that startup seminar and now like this… at the pool when you seem almost sloshed," asked Neil, completely perplexed.

"Yes, I know you very well. I know you since your story in *Messed Up! But All For Love* was published."

"That's not at all even closer to knowing me. That's more like fan following."

"I am your fan, if you allow me to…." Rachel had begun to slur. The lights faded away. Neil politely left, ensuring he escorted her to her room.

Before Neil could leave the spot, Rachel asked him to listen to her. She was adamant.

"Look Neil, I do not know whether I'll get a chance to talk to you or meet you again. I don't know whether you will even accept my business proposal. So for now, I want to let it all be personal. No business to be mixed in friendship. And since I am your fan, I need to tell you everything that matters. Are you listening to me, Neil? Oh, what does Gauri call you? My Neil? Man! What a lovely letter she wrote for you! You know Neil, that's what I like about you. Are you listening to me, Gauri's Neil? Are…?"

"Yes, Gauri. Oh I mean Rachel. Yes I am… all ears… but I have to go soon. I came here to change my clothes," Neil said in an evident hurry to get away.

Rachel looked at Neil from head to toe.

"See, that's what I love about you. You are here with me. I am hot and you have all the freedom to hit on me, and yet you are missing your wife so much. That really makes me wet… you know, like in real. I am a spoilt girl, that's why men leave me. They can't handle so much fire inside me. But they come to me first. They ogle at me. They strip me with their eyes. I can see that. Now when I see you, I find the reason why you are still stable with a woman, despite your scandal with Drishti. By the way, Neil, don't lie to me if I ask you to tell me did you not hump Drishti? Tell me, Neil. I promise it will be sssshhhhhhhh… I won't talk about it. Tell me… tell me…" she literally held Neil by his shirt and shook him. She was normal in her speech, yet the stuff she said gave Neil the idea that the next day, Rachel wouldn't remember a thing.

"Rachel, you know what… if you were not Mehr's friend, I might have even thrown you in the pool." Neil was frustrated to the point of screaming. He simply left the spot.

Rachel retired into her room. She did not chase Neil. The fact of the matter was that she had no energy left to run or even walk. She rushed into her room, threw her heels, and went to the minibar. She picked a bottle of Corona and looked at it before opening it with her teeth.

"Hey bitch, hope you cool me down!"

She lay on the bed and gulped a few sips, pouring the rest down her face.

"Neil, I am coming for you man. I love guys who do not sleep around. Like the ones who don't get tamed. You are a fiercely loyal and loving man. It's not going to be easy, but one day, I will tame you. How can you avoid me? Phew! You said you will throw me into the pool thinking I am sloshed. Hahaha, you've got to see me now. And don't take me wrong man. I am just looking for a lovely friendship. Nothing else. But I love you, man. Goodnight Mehr and Tom. Goodnight Neil."

She sank into her slumber.

Back at the venue, Sreedhar and Alicia had been happily talking with Neil and Gauri.

"This is our second meeting, right?" asked Sreedhar.

"Abbey yaar, could have been the third, but last time when we guys had planned Cuba, you had gone to Russia. Remember?"

"Yes yes, I remember." Sreedhar said.

"Hahaha, yes of course I remember too." Alicia chirped in. "And now, you have to come again to Cuba as we have big plans to launch the book in your presence," said Alicia.

Tom and Mehr also joined the gang. Most of the folks had left for the day. Only the friends lingered on. The guys split up and the women had their own agenda to catch up on.

As Neil lit up his Marlboro, Tom immediately burst out, "*Saaley yaad hai wo raat* when we were smoking and drinking in your DLF phase 4 apartment and throwing stubs and counting them. *Bahut pee thee yaar.*"

"Oh hell! Yes, I remember that night. Man, those days! A lot has changed. Look at this man – he's married again…" Neil said pointing at James.

"Come on, you guys haven't stopped pulling my leg. Finally I have married the right person," said James.

"Yes it took you three marriages to realize that the fourth one is the right one. Wow James, wow!"

"No idiots. It took me a few trips to India to realize that my love belongs here."

"Ya right," said Mehr laughing.

"Mehr, we thought it is our James who is the snoop dog. Didn't know you are kind of listening to us from such a distance," said Neil.

"Oho, you guys are talking so loudly. We are not eavesdropping," said Mehr, showing a punch to Tom.

"But baby, Neil said it. I am simply quiet," said Tom looking at Neil with a disapproving smile.

"Tom, welcome to the club. Forget your old gold days. Being single is different. Now you'll be blamed, no matter what," said Sreedhar.

Everyone erupted in laughter. That's what was bound to happen when friends gather. It's been some time that they all met like this. And these relationships can't be compared. The numbers could be counted. They were four couples. That's all. They would have more than a hundred friends combined. But tonight they were just eight. Eight close friends. When friends' friends become your friends and then you form a close circle, you will realize that the number would be not very high. It's rare for a hundred friends of yours to be friends with each other. That was being witnessed that night.

The atmosphere was all charged up. The talks would go on and celebrations were bound to continue.

"Listen, singlehood reminds me – who is that girl named Rachel? I bloody did not see her in the entire reception and now I bumped into her by the pool," asked Neil looking at Tom with much curiosity.

"Who… Rachel? Listen Mehr, now Neil wants to know about Rachel. Kindly enlighten our friend," Tom said out aloud unexpectedly.

Neil was completely embarrassed and he could be seen lip syncing abuses one after the other.

Mehr excused herself as Gauri was in a deep discussion with Alicia. Maybe they were discussing the plan for the travels and the launch. Or perhaps a shopping spree was on the cards.

As Mehr approached Neil, he was trying to hide his embarrassment.

"Neil, I know she is my college friend and we have remained in touch off and on, but she is way too flamboyant for you to be friends with. And I mean it. Why are you so quiet? Sorry, I didn't even ask you what happened."

Neil explained it all to her. Mehr gave him the complete picture of her background, her life and every small detail that would help. Neil began to recollect a few episodes of her that had come out in the print media. He remembered her at a few parties featured in Page 3 as well.

Some points were absorbed, some were casually overlooked and whatever did not make sense was happily ignored. The cocktails did the magic. It was a wonderful night that they would cherish for a long time to come.

Tom and Mehr left for Tashkent for their honeymoon the next day. Alicia and Sreedhar stayed back. James went off on a Rajasthan tour with Sagorika, his bong wife.

Neil and Gauri stayed put. They were on their kid planning mission.

It was a typical weekday where you can expect fireworks at the work place. Monday had gone two days ago and the weekend was two days away. One was bang in the middle of the work week. It sucked! Neil's work-life balance had been screwed up for the past couple of weeks. So he wasn't in the right frame of mind. Come Wednesday and there was a goof up that had taken place. His office was on the fourteenth floor of Infinity Towers. That was the prime location in the suburbs of the national capital. His cabin was huge and it had a couple of couches, a refrigerator, wine shelf and even a kitchenette in the enclosure. Considering the job he was doing, managing APAC market for one of the world's largest cola manufacturers, this office was one of the perks apart from several others that included two annual company paid holidays, a luxury sedan, among several others.

For the last few days, the perks didn't seem to matter too much to him. At this stage of his life, when he was planning a family with his wife, all he needed was peace of mind and time to himself. He fixed up drinks with Tom as he had returned from his honeymoon. He desperately needed to vent it out.

The meeting was fixed at Hard Rock Cafe. Neil left the office early. Of course he was in no mood to continue his day till late after a verbal spat with his boss. The evening was good in terms of the weather. It wasn't as rough as one would have expected.

"Thankfully, something in life is good. If not the job, the weather is," Neil said to himself while waiting for his friend to turn up. It wasn't a long wait and Neil as always was there before time.

"You tell the waiter what we want, *yaar*. I am in no fuckin' mood to talk to any stranger anywhere in this world now," said Neil as soon as Tom pulled up a chair.

"*Abey shaadi meri hui hai,* and you are the one frustrated."

"*Meri ho rakhi hai na…*"

"*Locha kya hua wo bol…*"

"See I tell you, feminism *ke naam par* and diversity *ke naam par ye* hiring women is a stupid idea. They just want to hire women, no matter what. I had selected this guy who bloody has the merit and has solid candidature, but no!" continued Neil.

"Damn, I got ya. Then what happened?"

"Nothing. I got furious and it escalated. The rest is history. Tell me what do I do in this case?"

"*Kya karega?* I mean, *kya kar sakta hai tu*…you can forget it and move on?"

"I know that, but I showed my middle finger to my boss, and since then, it's gotten worse."

"Neil, what the fuck! Were you abusive too?"

"I abused him a hundred times in my head and just told him to fuck off in real."

"Hasn't he fired you yet?"

"Let him try… I won't spare him. But there is no point. I want to do my own thing now."

"Listen, bloody asshole, you let the opportunity go waste in my wedding reception. That Rachel can do something for you. She is a filthy rich lass."

"So you're sure that I've got to leave this job now?"

"Yes, am very much certain."

Tom reminded the steward to expedite their order. They were regulars with their Bacardi white rum and coke and their favourite sea food platter. Three drinks was routine, twice a month. This was an exceptional scenario and hence the evening would probably extend a bit longer. After a couple of drinks, Neil began to ease up a bit.

"Tom, look... I got no problem in reaching out to Rachel, but she was way too touchy and feely. That's all."

"She's like that, but she will be able to help you out if you want to start something of your own. You keep that level of understanding. I won't recommend her, but your situation today demands that you get your own startup going," said Tom.

"Hmmm... ya I shall also think of alternatives, but ya, I certainly can't work there anymore," said Neil.

Present day

Alicia and Sreedhar were chasing Carlos like crazy. It went to the extent that Carlos stopped attending to their calls. This frustrated and irritated the former. They went to the media to make an appeal for the first time, and it went viral in a matter of minutes.

The headlines ran strongly across the channels and their appeal caught the interest of the nation. It was Alicia who appealed to the nation.

"They had come here because we had invited them to our beautiful Caribbean nation. Little had we known that crime still exists to the extent that someone tried to kill them. One of us or some of us were involved in this heinous crime. We have not even been able to find them till now. We don't know where they are. We know there is a huge reward on finding them, and hence it would have interested some of you. My fellow country people, please look around your neighbourhood. If you find anything suspicious, please inform us. Please do. I beg of you with folded hands."

Then Alicia held out Neilakshi's photo.

"She is their little girl. She is only five and she doesn't even know anything yet. Our heart goes out to them."

Within fifteen minutes of the appeal, Carlos was transferred to another city. A new officer named Juan took over immediately. Carlos was asked to join the new city the next week and help Juan with the handover in the interim. He was completely flustered, but he had no option.

Sreedhar thanked Alicia for coming out with this strategy. Despite the heavy incessant rainfall, the media had gathered in the town and the couple addressed them with passion. Afterwards, they left in search of the couple, risking their lives.

Meanwhile, Alicia also kept calling Dhanya frantically and told her that the situation on the ground was just not normal. Till this time, Dhanya wasn't aware of Mehr's conversation with Gauri. She was told of Carlos's transfer and Dhanya didn't seem too happy with that decision. She assured Alicia that it was just a matter of time that the case would get solved.

"Look Alicia, we are covering all possible angles. We are currently questioning suspects here. Give me some time. Carlos or no Carlos, this will be solved. Just pray we find Gauri and Neil soon."

Alicia didn't react much and told Dhanya to keep her posted. And vice versa.

❖

Back in India – few hours ago

Inspector Tambe sought Dhanya's time for an important discussion. She obliged. They met at the cafe near Jehangir Art Gallery. The place was decided by Dhanya.

Tambe saluted her on meeting and they took the corner seat.

"Bolo Tambe ji, kya information laaye ho?" (Tell Tambeji, what information do you have?"

"Kaafi important news hai ma'am. I have almost got a breakthrough in Rahul Sood's suicide, ma'am. I think that might be of great interest to you," said Tambe with confidence.

Dhanya was patiently listening to him. Tambe was all set to make some startling revelations. Before he could speak further, Dhanya told him that she was on the task of investigating the disappearance of Neil and Gauri and therefore she won't be able to give him much time as far as Rahul's suicide was concerned.

"Ma'am, I understand that. But I want to ask you if you could get a search warrant for Rachel," Tambe opened up.

"What? On what basis? She is bloody powerful and you know that," snapped Dhanya.

"We are talking of a case of abetment of suicide and a possible money laundering angle here. And Rachel is involved in it."

"Wait, what? You have inferred that, Tambeji?"

"Yes ma'am, so naturally this will now move to CBI and, therefore, you."

Tambe disclosed all the facts based on whatever they could find from Rahul Sood's laptop, cellphone and even bank transactions. He was seemingly depressed for the last few days. It appeared that he was under huge pressure. The initial findings suggested that he was lured into it to make big money. But once he got involved, he was sucked in it. There was no way out for him. And he had even exchanged emails with Rachel for the same.

Also, two days before he killed himself, he was on a one hour long call with Vidhi. Most of his phone calls in the recent roles were with someone in Russia and Tashkent. The phone call records did not suggest any link to Rachel though. There was not a single phone call made between the two. That was surprising.

"Tambe ji, could you let me know if you checked the I.P. address of Rachel's email address? What was the trace and location?"

"No, we did not have that much time. But the email address was hers."

"Okay, don't worry. I shall take over the case from here on. Be ready for sleepless nights ahead. I shall get the search warrant for Rachel soon. Anything else you want to share with me?"

While Tambe scratched his head, Dhanya received a whatsapp from Vidhi.

'Dhanya ma'am. I am so sorry. I left without informing anyone. But you got to know that I love my boss a lot and hence I came here to Moscow.'

Dhanya immediately called her back. She got insights from Vidhi. The latter mentioned details of her last conversation with Rahul Sood.

"Ma'am, what do you plan to do now?"

"Vidhi, I am capable of discretion here. You tell me all that you have on you. Will you?"

"Rahul Sood was involved in money laundering for someone named V. That's how he addressed himself as. The call would always come from Moscow. He made some money and then got involved in it deeply. When he stopped taking his calls, he was threatened. Then, someone came to his house. Rahul was scared to death. He started taking leaves from work. I could see that difference in his behaviour as he would mostly have his coffee breaks with me. Then I thought of telling Neil about it, but he told me if I tell anyone, they would kill his family."

"Hey Vidhi, any clue why anyone would approach someone from Neil's company? Does Rachel have any connection to this?"

"That I don't know as he never told me about Rachel."

"Ok look, I got to go now. Keep your phone charged. And I believe you have to return to India. It's not safe for you. You never know your phone might be getting tapped. This seems to be a big trap."

"I was able to get help from one of my friends and he told me a lot more. His uncle worked in KGB and he told me that there are lot of shell companies that operate here and do this money laundering business."

"You did not have to go all the way to Moscow for that. Anyway, it's your decision. But be safe."

While they finished the call, Tambe confirmed the email address could be traced back to Moscow and it was just crusted to reflect as Rachel to divert attention. This was bizarre and complicated on the face of it, however to a CBI officer, it was worthy to explore, and hence, the search warrant for Rachel was coming.

Dhanya called up Vidhi again and told her that they would search her house as well. Vidhi was okay and added, "Please don't judge me if you find Neil's photographs in my browser history while I googled him. For the records, I can say that I am his assistant, so I am doing my job. In reality, I adore him."

Dhanya grinned.

"Tambe ji, this would definitely lead to somewhere that you and I cannot think right now. Let's get going."

They immediately headed to Vidhi's house. Till such time, the search warrant for Rachel arrives, they would have figured something from Vidhi's.

First and foremost, they took charge of the laptop. It contained huge data and therefore several files and videos. Two teams were formed to scan it completely. There was a Webex video recording that caught the attention of the cops. Its scanning revealed a conversation that had taken place between Rachel and some guy in broken English accent, where she was talking about executing the plan. It was a mere coincidence that the Webex recording was a result of a video call between Rachel and Vidhi when they were talking about work. During the discussion, the man from Russia had called Rachel. She did not turn the share video option off. The Webex recording option remained on and it captured the conversation, which revealed some ugly truths.

"Hi V, I am all set to have the plan executed. I am hoping I shall get the full contract. I am traveling to Moscow next week. Any questions you have for me?"

The other side of the conversation was not heard in the recording so far. However, the speaker phone was turned on at this stage by Rachel so it helped them a big deal.

V began to respond.

"From now onwards, please do not call me. Use the code word Isabella and we will take it forward from here and discuss the future of the deal. Your money will be moved to the account here. The details of the bank account shall flash on your phone for one minute and then it will be automatically erased. Do not save it. Just memorize it. That is all for now. I got to go."

The cops had noted all the points and were ready to interrogate Rachel. Also, the Interpol sent out details to the seniors, of the investigation that they had done jointly with the Cuban police. There were a hundred raids that were conducted in the past twenty-four hours across the country. At least Havana was 100% scanned. There were about a hundred and ten registrations or places or something that were linked to Isabella. The bank accounts of all the individuals associated were taken control of. All the phone call details of these individuals were analyzed.

Here in Artemisa, Valencia's husband was glued to the television. Upon seeing his son's photo as one of the suspects, he became alert. As he watched the news of the transfer followed by the statement from Alicia, he immediately got up and shared the information with both the ladies.

It did strike Gauri to inform Alicia immediately, but she consulted Valencia,

"Auntie, I don't know why, but I don't trust anyone. Please don't take me wrong. But it's only you in this country that I trust. You know our plan of going to watch the food festival was only known to Alicia and Sreedhar. They did not know the place, I believe, or I don't remember telling them. Oh gosh! What is wrong with me? I am not even trusting friends. I don't know whether I am right or wrong, but I am way too guarded. Hope this is fine, auntie?"

"Yes Gauri. It is absolutely fine. Now that top cop has also been transferred. Don't know what they are doing. But they will not be able to close the investigation till they find you."

Before Gauri could respond, there were loud gunshots. Due to the thunderstorm and rains, the residents could not figure what they were.

Gauri got slightly panicked as she feared it was some attack. Ricardo also sensed it wasn't normal thunder. He tried to peep out and suddenly dodged a bullet that crossed his window. He alerted the ladies and rushed towards his gun.

Due to the flooded roads, it was not easy for the attackers to continue shooting. The house was about five to six feet higher than the ground level. The flat ground was already flooded with rainwater. There was no stairwell from outside. And the water had made everything slippery, including the water pipes. Despite all this, it seemed they were professionals. Rather, it was surely hardcore criminals on the job.

They were shooting from all corners of the house, targeting the windows, and all the open vents. It appeared that it would be impossible for the occupants of the house to survive. They were about a dozen in number and were attired in complete black. It was clear that the idea was to kill everyone.

Every time there was a shot, one knew that it represented a life. They were scared to death. Ricardo ran across the window and stood to the side. He had an advantage that he was not standing in the flood and was at a height. He took aim and killed one man. That was the perfect aim from the hunter. He knew the best place now would be to reach the terrace. However, he wanted to also secure the remaining three occupants. The furore wouldn't die down anytime soon. There were too many of them. It seemed endless.

Gauri and Valencia lifted Neil and ran upstairs. It seemed much safer up there.

This time around, half a dozen men started shooting at the main door as they had managed to cross the flood and reach it. They somehow managed to break open the door. The house was pitch dark as Ricardo had intelligently pulled out the main fuse. The moment they opened the door, water gushed in and that kind of swept them off their feet in the dark. No matter how professional they were, it was not easy to fight against nature. Or it was god who was on the side of the family!

What Valencia had also smartly done was that she had poured oil on the stairwell inside that led to the rooms upstairs. Like they say, chance favours the prepared mind.

The gun shots were loud inside the house. Ricardo held his gun at the top in the room, ready to fire. Simultaneously, Gauri and Valencia attempted calling the cops again, and finally, Valencia was able to connect to them. Juan was present and took stock of the situation. Juan told her that the team was almost there as they had tracked their whereabouts. Carlos, during the handover, had mentioned the location to him. Andres must have delivered the key info. Two men made their way up, but fell miserably on their face due to the oil. Ricardo shot them dead. He was bang on target. The others left in the room changed their course. They tried to move out and join the other members who were on the other side of the house. Ricardo sensed that and took position on the terrace. He shot dead two more. The shooters thought there were more people in the house covering the place and hence could not attack freely.

It was indeed quite scary for the women. Amidst the action, Neil gained some consciousness. He kept calling out to Gauri a few times. He was even able to move his hands. Gauri didn't know how to react. She sat down on the ground while Neil lay on the bed. She knew there was clear danger, yet she could not avoid displaying what she was going through. Her emotions were boundless. She caressed him, held his head and with her face, rubbed his. Her tears were dropping on Neil's face. He was able to communicate now. It was probably the shock and the gun shots that helped him regain consciousness. That is what she had thought. It was the wife's dedication and love for her husband that was most prominent and visible. Even in the darkness. Love doesn't care about the timing and circumstances. It just shines anywhere, in any form, provided the souls connect with each other. So were theirs, shining and gloriously making their presence felt. Gauri hugged her husband and kept talking to him. He was responding intermittently in whispers. It was only a matter of time when the cops would turn up in full battalion. Ricardo had shot six of them and the cops chased the rest who fought back. None of them survived, though Juan wanted to catch them alive. One hell of an unexpected night came to an end.

The days to come would reveal the ugly truth. In the perfect world, Neil would heal and Gauri would be able to lead a wonderful life again. Well, that's where life keeps testing you. One the one hand you plan something, and on the other, it is snatched away. Life can alter its course. Anytime.

A new step – When Neil switched over

Neil took a week off from office. He wanted to use this time to set his life straight. Or at least try something new. He was in two minds in the beginning. He and Gauri were planning to begin a family now, and were looking forward to having a child, the confirmation of which would come in a few days. On the other hand, he would have to leave the job and take a risk with the startup. Whatever the case may be, it wasn't going to be easy.

He had not shared his ordeal with Gauri yet. Maybe he felt that he could handle it on his own or with the help of Tom. But that wouldn't last long. If he had to approach Rachel, there was no way for him not to confide in Gauri. There was no auspicious day in the calendar that would automatically show up and guide Neil to initiate things.

One evening, Gauri asked Neil to pick her up from the supermart as her car was at the garage. He had all the time in the world to do the errands or fetch his wife and anything else. Gauri couldn't understand it at first. However, that evening, she asked him if everything was alright, like a concerned wife.

"Your life has been fucked up at work and you are telling me now, Neil? Bloody hell, *biwi hu tumhari*. And all these years have gone by, but you are still the same. First you will tell Tom and then you tell me, only after I insist," said an upset looking Gauri, for obvious reasons.

"Oho Gauri, you are almost about to be pregnant and so I didn't want to trouble you. I don't think this is anything serious. It can be easily handled," said Neil.

"Neil, being almost pregnant doesn't mean that you won't share your thoughts with me. In fact, if I do get pregnant, then I would need a lot of care from you. And yes, a lot of openness and honesty also, my Neil. Come now." She hugged him.

"Look, I wanted to tell you that now I am planning to start my own thing."

"Go ahead. I am there with you for anything."

"Thanks darling. I will do it through that girl we talked about, Rachel. The owner of Trust Cements and Steel."

"Oh that friend of Mehr, I remember. So Tom is convinced about her?"

"He firmly believes she can help me out. And if need be, Mehr can put in a word."

"Then go for it. Don't dilly dally. I want your happiness. And don't be the least bothered about anything."

Relationships are like fruits. You can never be sure about the sweetness till you dive into it. You can still try to judge it from the outside. Like look at the skin, shape, size, fragrance and be carried away. But until you bite it, or taste it, you won't know. Neil and Gauri were in the same boat. They had tasted the fruit of relationship and knew the sweetness of it. Gauri reflected just that. She was by her husband's side like a strong pillar.

"Honey, do you know I love you like penguins do?"

"Hahaha. I know, you had told me the penguin story. "

His favourite true fact about penguins was that when a male penguin falls in love with a female penguin, he searches the entire beach to find the perfect pebble to present to her. And when he finally finds it, he waddles over her and places the pebble right in front of her. It is kind of a proposal. Neil always compared his love with this story.

The next day, Neil reluctantly reached office. He was to attend a critical meeting. Despite his leave, he preferred to go, so as to not drop any clues of his dissatisfaction. To his surprise, he received a closed envelope that did not have the name of the sender on it. However, on opening it, there was an offer from Rachel.

Dear Neil,

Let's work it out. Call me at 022-73211982 at your convenience. I promise you won't regret it.

Sincerely yours, thanks

R

"And the 'R' has to be you, Rachel. Just last night I was talking to Gauri about you. And here you are. Wow Tom, you got to have pumped her," Neil said to himself.

In a natural rush, immediately after the office meeting he called up Rachel.

"Hello Rachel."

"Hi Neil. So glad you called."

"My apologies for the other day. I don't know what I said, but I didn't mean it."

"I don't think you even uttered a word. I was the one talking."

"Ohhhh, so you don't remember much?"

"That I offered you a business deal and then you dropped me to my room and I offered you coffee and you said politely that you had to leave. I believe you and I had a coffee and then you asked me to get in touch with you, and so I did that today," said Rachel.

"Oh yes, I remember. Coffee. Yes. Ya... it was nice. What's next now?" Neil faked it on purpose.

"Please come down to my Mumbai office on Saturday and we shall take it forward from there."

"Thanks Rachel."

"My pleasure, Neil. I am waiting for you with bated breath."

Neil was delighted and called up Tom to thank him, who feigned ignorance. He maintained that she did it all on her own.

"But what is so interesting about me, I still don't understand? I mean, reading about my life in a book made her so mad that she now wants me to start my company with her support?"

"Bro, she is like that. Mehr told me once she liked a guy in the college, and on his birthday, she gifted him a BMW."

"Tom, I am taking a chance, but my instinct asks me to go for it."

❖

She had a plush office, as expected. It was a sea-facing building at Nariman Point. The tower was called Rachel Towers. It was a landmark to quite a few places around. Considering Nariman Point houses top business houses, to stand out was noteworthy. Her forefathers had made it there after lot of slogging and hard work. Today, she was heading the international bottling division of her company as a Managing Director. It was capped at USD 700 million. The steel was still managed by her father and that business was worth two billion USD. Overall, the family was worth three plus billion.

Rachel had been planning to expand into South Africa and was eyeing an acquisition that would make her a billion dollar worth. Neil worked in a similar field and she had that connect with him. Somehow she knew he could be trusted if left independent. When her father asked why she couldn't select someone from her existing team, she was quite firm and maintained that as an independent director, she held the right to make her decisions, even though his views were welcome. At twenty-three, when she took over the business, it was 200 million dollar worth. In seven years, it grew to 700 million USD, and now the target of one billion USD in next two years seemed realistically possible. Provided Neil agreed.

After a customary welcome, Rachel and Neil sat in the lounge that was the area meant for her personal visitors. At the outset, the businesswoman in front of him and the lady who Neil encountered at Tom's reception were two different people.

There was not an iota of doubt on that front. So it was evident that Rachel kept her professional and personal life different. Neil was quite convinced about her and the initial discussion went fine.

"What's your notice period, Neil?"

"Three months and there are no hidden clauses."

"What's your expected remuneration?"

"I am looking for a more independent role, and close to a 7-8 crore per annum, plus perks."

"Here is the offer for you, Neil. You are going to be a partner in the firm with high stakes. I am hoping you'll love it."

"You prepared my offer letter without asking how much I earn? And by the way, thank you for everything."

While Neil opened it, he was still unsure as to why this was happening with him. Maybe he was highly skilled for the role and the firm belief of the founders in him was acting like a magnet. Or was there something else that he didn't know at this point?

Neil was given the date of 1st October to join. And the first assignment would be in South Africa.

He broke the news to Tom and Gauri and was on the way to resign within hours.

The weather gods seemed quite happy with this belt of the Delhi suburbs. The afternoon turned dark as the clouds enveloped the skies and swirled overhead. They turned the dark gloomy thunderous atmosphere into a cheerful rainy day.

Neil decided to write a song for Gauri who would join him at any moment.

Just look at the skies
Look at the colours
Look at the water falling down
And the greens smiling all the way

Now I need to feel your skin
As the breeze fills my senses
I need you to come to me
As the rains splash up a cheer

Look at the prism of light
That finds its way through the grey skies
Look at the clouds playing around
And the palms waving in joy

Now I want you to kiss me all over
Like the rains kissing the palms
Like the clouds kissing the skies
And the evening kissing the nights.

He was completely absorbed in the beautiful and enticing evening, now joined by his equally beautiful wife. Gauri came with cups of coffee and the mug was etched with twins and a message 'Happy mommy and daddy'.

She came with an unusual smile and sat on his lap after showing off the mugs with a pointed finger. She raised her eyebrows and both of them exchanged notes in silence. Neil was running the song in his mind, which he now believed could have had the touch of a baby in it. So he decided to add four additional lines so that when he sang it, there would be a holistic appeal to it and would definitely make it more complete.

There was an automatic transition. From the normal Gauri-oriented, romantic, loyal husband to a family man who had started thinking about his kids. Twins were in consideration and anticipation.

Neil held Gauri by her shoulders and sang the song with lines included about the children.

"And lastly these four lines to welcome our kids," he said.

We looked up in the skies and asked god
And he fulfilled our wish and gifted us
With such lovely and beautiful kids
That we need nothing else and feel so complete.

"Wow, Neil you keep surprising me all the time. And I cannot believe that you guessed correctly about your wife being pregnant. You know I wanted to surprise you tonight, but you know it already, man."

Neil did not know about Gauri's pregnancy. He had to let the feeling sink in. More importantly, he had to continue behaving like he knew. He did not want to break the feeling at any given point. His wife was expecting a lot from him.

"Gauri, can you just let me sit down and feel our child move?"

"Oh baby, it's too early for that."

"I know honey, yet I want to kiss your tummy, for there is a life in it. Our love is blooming inside of you. Inside your blood stream. A life is shaping. You and I in a new form altogether."

The night had crawled upon them and the air had turned chilly. It did not feel like the summers anymore. The temperature had dropped down to fifteen degree Celsius. The coffee had turned cold. From the song to the touch to the moments of bliss – they were moments that you would dream of as a family.

Gauri looked at him and remained silent for a bit and then asked Neil to sit beside her so she could put her head on his lap.

"Baby, let me get up and warm the coffee again. We did not realize the weather would freeze it so quick," said Gauri.

"Look, you sit back and relax. Don't do too much running around. I'll do it."

Neil got up and walked to the kitchen.

He could mildly hear Gauri saying something and tried to guess what it was. She was telling him it was okay to let her work as she didn't need rest until the last month.

"Yeah, I hear you. Need to buy literature and understand the subject well," said Neil.

He was back in no time and the couple resumed their chat. They needed to plan a lot for the future now.

"You know, the kid is lucky for us. I even landed a new job offer."

"Yeah, and that too a hugely significant jump."

"You are happy?"

"Yes, of course, my Neil. Our life is changing now. I am happy to see my man growing in life. I am thrilled beyond comprehension to bear our child. I just knock on wood. Hope nothing goes wrong."

"No way, Gauri. Nothing will go wrong."

"I want our love to be like this. I hear people talk about love diminishing after the child is born and all that. I tell you, to me, you are most important, and then comes the child. You hear that, Neil. I can't lose you."

"My baby, come to me. Let me hug you. And you know why do you get so emotional now? Because of the hormonal changes in your body," Neil said as he was reading something on the internet on his mobile phone.

"Haha, my Google doctor. Stop that! Ask me for any literature."

As they sipped their coffee, the doorbell rang. Tom and Mehr were at the door.

"*Waah Neil waah, honeymoon par hum gaye and papa tum ban rahe ho?*" said Mehr with a laugh as she placed the bouquet in the vase beside the television.

"Look at his face glowing. And blushing."

Tom pinched Neil's back as he reached the balcony. Gauri had stood up and began to walk inside the living room.

"Gauri, stay there. The weather is blessing us today," said Mehr.

"Okay, listen Mehr, get an extra cushion from the couch."

Both the couples sat in the balcony. One had returned from their honeymoon and the other had taken a leap towards a new journey.

"So finally, Rachel found the guy she needed to steer her business with. You know, she had been looking for someone for a long time, but I still can't believe she was eyeing Neil, our great man," Mehr chuckled.

"Ya, all that is fine, but I hope you haven't told anyone else about the pregnancy."

Mehr looked at Tom as she was certain about herself. In return, he appeared completely confused, "Look Mehr, Neil texted me. I told ya, you confirmed with Gauri, and after that, we both decided to leave. On the way, you picked the bouquet which took you three minutes, without any bargaining. I was turning the car when that happened and then you came with the flowers. So net net, where was any indication of me sharing the news with anyone?" said Tom in a furiously calm manner.

"Neil, after our marriage, look how Tom has transformed. I did not say anything and look at his lengthy Nehru type speech," said Mehr.

"But your expressions said it na," said Tom.

"Okay guys, truce. The topic at hand is how was your honeymoon and our parenthood. Let's not digress. Let's only progress. *Waah waah*, I'm rhyming," laughed Gauri.

The night was carefree, unfolding brilliantly. Magnificent to the core. Everlasting brotherhood and friendship, with no superficially inclined smiles and behaviour. That's what kept them going.

Music played in the background. Bonds continued to strengthen. Neil told them about his date of joining and plans to be in South Africa for a month to settle things. Gauri would be four months pregnant then. Mehr would continue with the regular support, apart from the normal house help. In addition, Neil's mom was coming over too. All was set.

Time flies. Like they say. It only seemed like yesterday. It was the end of September. In just a few days, Neil was to move to Mumbai. A couple of weeks there before he would fly to Cape Town.

While he made the preparations, Gauri was feeling extremely uneasy. More emotionally and mentally, than physically. She hadn't been in this situation before, where she felt so vulnerable and insecure. Neil tried explaining to her, however it was understood that she would take her own time to feel alright.

"Look, I want to come along. There is no point for us to trouble mom or anyone else for that matter, okay?"

She knew even though she made that statement, there was still confirmation that she needed from Neil as she did not want him to feel encumbered with additional responsibility while he was on a big mission.

"Honey, I would love for us to be together all the time, but please understand there is so much travel that is planned for the coming days. You know it all. Why unnecessarily go through the hassle?"

Gauri sat in the corner. Her eyes were moist. She looked at the ground, folded her hands, and began sobbing softly.

Neil held her in his arms and kept comforting her, yet remained quite practical.

"How will I live without you for so long?"

"Honey, it's just a matter of forty-five days and that's all about it. There's FaceTime. We'll see and speak to each other every day, and that's my promise. You won't feel I am away. Time flies. You know that too."

"Neil, last time if you remember what had happened when I had gone to Chennai for a week. I feel whenever we stay apart, there is some bloody curse. I am not feeling good yet again."

"Relax baby. You are overthinking. If it were an ordinary trip to a new country in my existing job, I would have not even thought twice. This is a new beginning, a partnership in a big company. There's ambiguity at this point, which means there is lots for me to do. Hence it makes perfect sense—" said Neil.

Gauri remained uneasily quiet for some more time. Then she asked Neil to help her get up and then she hugged him. The tears did burst out. She was holding on to them for way too long, but felt lighter afterwards.

She would soon have the company of Neil's mother.

It was Friday, the 29th of September, 2017. Neil would join his new office on Tuesday, the 3rd of October. He wanted to settle down by the weekend.

"Mom, please take care of yourself and Gauri. She has really become over sensitive and I did read in the books that it's natural and normal for her to feel so," said Neil.

He was given the assurance by his mother. She mentioned that it is absolutely fine and okay for her to feel this way. She would ensure that Gauri would only feel loved and secure.

Gauri, in the meantime, wrote a letter for Neil.

Dearest Neil,

It has been more than a decade that we have been together. In this marital world bound by love and affection, you have been the best guy on the planet for me. You have been the best human being, rather. I have never felt so hollow before as I feel now. It is not because you make me feel so or anything that either you or I are responsible for, it is rather the way we have dealt with certain situations in the past that makes me go crazy. I know you love me and you know I love you more and that shall always stay. I understand our principles of love – to stick to the basics and the core and to only focus on love and care. I shall do so. I shall wait for you till eternity. I shall be here, longing for you, for your touch, for that is what I will miss more. I shall miss those lovely times that we spend together, those morning songs and that morning love we so much cherish. Gosh! My Neil, come back soon, for it is not so easy to write all this. I know I have goofed up this time around while writing to you, however I know that you understand why it is so. You would have figured it on Google by now that because I am pregnant, I am not acting normal in any way.

Neil, I love you now and forever and beyond. Come back soon.

xoxo

Love,

Gauri

❖

It took him an hour to reach his office from Leela Kempinsky, where he would stay for another week. He carried two large bags. His apartment was not yet ready. So this was his temporary dwelling and temporary car, driven by the office chauffeur. Mumbai had some memories from the past which were bitter-sweet. It was here where he was arrested a couple of years ago. And that was at Pizza by the Bay which was about a mile from his new office. He did overcome it, however, for just a moment, he did remember it. Cities and places are the best reminders of memories. People are mostly forgotten.

Neil made it fifteen minutes before the scheduled time for his breakfast meeting with Rachel. He decided to briefly call Gauri. "Hey baby, the journey has been good so far. I still find it surreal."

"Okay, Neil. Just give your best and keep me posted."

"How is your health now? Any pain?"

"No, I am normal. No kicking in my tummy yet. Hope to get that soon. You go now… unmm and don't worry, it's cool."

"Aha! That's great to hear. Please take care. And I love you and miss you."

As they bid each other goodbye, Neil reached his new work place. He was escorted to the office by Vidhi, his new secretary and soon to be confidante.

He was welcomed by the staff at the eleventh floor that literally held him and walked him along to Rachel's office. She had stepped out with a warm welcome gesture. She wore an

Armani suit and the Clive Christian No. 1 perfume, the fragrance of which could simply sweep anyone off their feet. Her high heeled Jimmy Choos made a thumping sound as they landed each time when she took those strides to welcome the man whom she had been waiting for with bated breath. Unexpected and unbelievable for Neil and his family.

With a broad smile, she shook hands and proactively stretched herself forward for a warm hug. She would usually replicate this with foreign delegates or anybody senior or somebody very close to her. Neil reciprocated equally with genuine gratitude that he felt and displayed.

The terms and conditions were already exchanged over emails and both were mutually in sync on the same. But that wasn't the agenda for the day. Rachel was very particular about everything. She ensured the travel plans were taken care of well and also that Neil should feel warmly welcomed. She reached work an hour early and personally oversaw his office.

They had an informal breakfast meeting together. Neil simply asked her how she appeared much taller than when he had last met her. Rachel was quick with a witty response, "When you saw me last, I was barefeet by the poolside in swimwear – too casual, too dark and too drunk… hahaha… you got me, right? I am different in the night and during the day. Hope that sounds simpler," she laughed hysterically.

Neil looked at her and carefully nodded. Rachel and Neil continued the discussion as the latter paid attention to the agenda for the week. After the wrap up, he was taken upstairs. He glanced across the corner plush office which was on the twelfth floor, a floor above hers. He was awestruck. His plush office gave him goosebumps. It was the size of his DLF apartment, almost. And certainly bigger than many of the apartments in Mumbai.

"Hello sir, I am Vidhi, your executive assistant." As Vidhi introduced herself, she took Neil around the office and explained everything in great detail. He was mighty impressed with her. She handed over the docket that contained tickets and itinerary for the South Africa trip over the coming weekend. After the formalities were executed through the day, Neil returned to his office window and talked to himself while looking outside at the skyscrapers.

"Neil, hope you are not moving too fast. Hope this is all fine. And the lady seems mysterious, mate. How come Mehr doesn't know all this secret side of hers? Maybe I am reading too much."

There was a knock on the door. It was Vidhi.

"What happened, sir? You appear to be in a pensive mood. If I may ask, is everything alright?"

"Vidhi, it's all fine. New place, new people, that's all. How long have you been here?"

"I complete two years next month. I was EA to the earlier CEO who moved on recently."

"Oh you're talking about Mr Datta? Why did he leave?"

Vidhi evaded the topic smartly. She subtly came near Neil and said, "I don't know, sir, what leads to resignations at the top level, but I can tell you with some belief that it is mostly driven by misunderstanding issues and disconnects. Why would a CEO who was highly paid leave for a sabbatical?"

"Yes, that's a good point. Thanks for the articulation. By the way, I truly appreciate your effort. Let me now settle in. I shall give you a buzz if I need anything."

The day was over and the coming days and weeks would bring about significant changes in the life of this man.

Air Seychelles was on time and so were its guests seated on 1A and 1B. Rachel was in her informal avatar. Over the last few days, she and Neil had spent a great deal of time together, talking about business. She knew how to switch from formal business affairs to a completely different avatar. She knew herself well. Did Neil know her even a tad bit? The answer was no. She was completely unpredictable.

Rachel was keen in knowing about Neil's past life. Whatever she had known of him was through the book, *Messed Up! But All For Love,* and therefore, she had many questions to ask. It was more than what a reader would ask an author. It was something much beyond her own comprehension. Neil slept after brief chats and gulping a couple of single malts. The discussion and answers to Rachel's questions would continue later.

Rachel looked closely at Neil and kept doing that without any break. She had downed a good amount of wine, to the point of melting her heart. Not just her heart, but all her senses were filled with something magical. She was trying to discover that. Every look at Neil, and she would smile and sip her wine. This continued. She was incessantly talking to herself.

"Neil, you are so handsome man. Why are you still with Gauri when she is only a troublemaker? I hope after this trip you are mine and only mine. And don't consider what I am doing for you to be any favour. Umm… it's a simple barter. I give you myself and this whole new life, and then all I want is you. All I need is you and your love. Neil, come on, get up and look at your future."

She got up from her seat and kissed Neil. Like a few times. She was unstoppable. Neil was dead asleep. He feared turbulence so it was his priority to quickly gulp down some alcohol and sleep through the flight. Rachel was not his priority.

Much of Rachel's desires were materializing. She had the man whom she had badly wanted. He had left his job and had joined her company. And she wanted to kiss him some day. And fly with him. All check marked so far. She wanted to make love to him and get him away from Gauri. She hated Gauri more than she actually loved Neil. That was the conflict.

The fourteen-hour long, sleepy for one and dreamy for the other, journey came to an end. The lovely port town of Cape Town welcomed them. They were staying at The Westin Cape Town which oversaw the harbour. They checked in around eight in the evening. Their rooms were on separate floors. Vidhi did the booking and the room numbers weren't allotted next to each other as one would have expected. It wasn't known if Rachel wanted it this way. At the reception, when the staff mentioned about their floor and room numbers, Rachel briefly glanced at Neil to check his expressions. He just asked for the corner room with a view. The staff obliged.

It was decided they'd meet for dinner at Thirty7 restaurant after half an hour. Neil called up Gauri and had a long chat with her before switching the mode to video. It was six in the evening India time, and Gauri was home early. Gauri told him how she was feeling like a mother now and how much she was missing him.

"You know Gauri, I am truly blessed to have a wife like you, who is so supportive and understanding."

"Neil, looks like you are missing your wife in just a few days of separation. If it gets tough for you considering you are there for at least a week or maybe more, I can fly down," said an emotional Gauri.

"In fact, Gauri, it's more because you are pregnant. Also, I somehow feel that when I am starting something new, I should have my wife with me. Let me mull it over and broach the subject with Rachel."

"Sounds cool. How is Rachel? Hope she is treating you fine."

"She is way too cool and balanced. At work, she is a thorough professional, and outside, she is a complete sport."

"Okay, all that is great, Neil. But Mehr was telling me again that after a few *daru* pegs or glasses, she loses control. Somewhere there was an issue between her and her previous CEO because of the same reason. Just be careful, though I know you can handle it well."

"Don't worry at all. In fact, she has even taken care of booking our rooms on separate floors."

"That's great. You look tired, Neil. Don't go anywhere. Just have your dinner and sleep. Mehr is coming over tonight. Mom has stepped out for evening bhajan in the neighborhood."

"Okay love. Bye now. Will call tomorrow."

Neil slipped into evening casuals after a nice hot water shower. It was a little past 9.30 p.m. He was all set for dinner where his host was waiting and walking in the lobby.

"So sorry, Rachel. I had to keep you waiting," said Neil with all humility.

"Are you usually so humble, Neil? You continue to impress me."

Before Rachel would expect a reaction from Neil, he came closer and pulled the chair to give Rachel the seat. She was mighty impressed. Not that she hadn't been around such men, but it was a different feeling to be treated like this by the one you were fond of. In fact, crazily fond of.

They ordered *bunny chow, chakalaka* for the main course and *malva* pudding and cheesecake for dessert. Drinks were avoided.

"Neil, I wanted to ask you something. When you worked in your previous firm, what was usually the sales force alignment to the prospective deal?"

Neil was quite normally explaining it and the business discussion continued.

"You know, we lost the last bid to them just because of the CEO I had hired. He goofed up," said Rachel.

Neil participated in the discussion with all passion till Rachel asked him some questions that would have meant giving out insider information if he still held his previous job.

"See, now you know how important you are to us. The rates you mentioned were pretty competitive. I am hoping you will bring all your expertise to the position. We are meeting the clients tomorrow and while I shall lead the main discussions, I would really want you to chime in when needed."

"First of all, I am glad that you find me so important, Rachel. Rest assured, will give it my best shot. Where is the meeting? I don't see the venue on the calendar."

"Oh yes, thanks for reminding me. Could you tell Vidhi to confirm it from David, our client partner, as he had told her to wait. I believe he would like to have a place that can impress his bosses. So much for clinching the deal, phew! Part of the game."

La Colombe was about twenty minutes from The Westin. It was one of the fine French style restaurants. Vidhi had chosen this after discussing it with the client representative. There was a dinner and discussion planned. There were few people from Rachel's team who would also be present.

At about 6.30 in the evening, two Rolls Royces had arrived. There were two more cars that followed and one that was ahead. This mini fleet had a layer of security cover for its guests.

This wasn't unprecedented. A year ago, it was almost like a grand event here. Rachel enjoyed this support and love from the government. And why wouldn't she – she was bringing in investment to the country and to this port town. Also, she had a good relation with the government here. There were two countries which prioritized on her list for business footprint and expansion. South Africa was one and Cuba was another. Once the bottling plant was set up here, she would want to focus her energy on some of the large construction projects in Cuba. Havana, to begin with. It wasn't confirmed whether that would roll up to Neil or she would be involved herself.

She came dot on time, accompanied by Neil. The latter was flabbergasted as he watched the security set up and the fleet of high luxury transportation. In the wildest of his dreams wouldn't he have imagined the aura that Rachel had and the life she lived. This was his first grand introduction to the lifestyle of the rich and famous.

"Hope you are comfortable, Neil?"

"I am more than comfortable and this beast looks like it belongs to the American president."

"Yes, you won't believe it, but this design is the replica and is fully bullet proof. You can imagine how important we become when we plan to invest a few hundred million dollars. And not just that, when your relationship with the government is great, this is considered normal hosting," said Rachel.

"Yes, I believe you. And I am mighty impressed. Tell me if you are my employer or my friend or my business partner?" asked Neil with curious looks.

"What does your offer letter say, dear?"

"It does not specify any of those things, except my compensation and perks that are being offered. And those are exorbitantly high, and my gratitude for that. To become a managing partner with you is probably the best thing," Neil said carefully, choosing his words humbly.

Rachel put her hand on Neil's and said, "You are more than just a friend or a business partner. Umm… look at you blushing. Come on Neil, a rich business tycoon telling you what you mean to her should make you fall on your knees… and there is ample space in this Royce."

"Aha, space for me to kneel down? You are so unpredictable, Rachel."

Rachel remained mysteriously quiet like she wanted Neil to keep speculating. On the other hand, Neil switched on his iPad and studied the reports further for a fruitful meeting.

The moment had arrived. La Colombe, one of South Africa's finest eateries, had snatched the seventh placed on the list of the World's Best Restaurants at the TripAdvisor Travellers Choice

Awards. The choice of place won the hearts of the clients and hosts alike. Neil held the fort and impressed the clients with his dynamic persona, knowledge and strategy.

A lot of the ground work had happened previously, however, after meeting the man who would lead the company into the future, their confidence was strengthened. The press brief was released and the media crew was ready with the bite for the next morning. The deal worth 300 million dollar worth of investment was announced. It was big news for the hungry media. Congratulations were exchanged. Facebook and Instagram live took place on various news channels.

Rachel had put her money on the right person. She hugged the man and thanked him for pulling off this big deal. The clients were happy and the agenda was set for the coming weeks.

The dinner went off excellently well and the evening was as good as it could be. Rachel decided to take Neil to a beach-side pub nearby. She was exhausted and wanted to celebrate privately with Neil. The latter was equally excited and left the place happily.

Rachel decided to go to Grand Africa Cafe and Beach where a table was already in place. Vidhi was excellent at her job. Rachel was predictive. All this was pre-decided. The setting was highly up class. And the two sweet looking people were living their dreams. Rachel was beyond ecstatic. Neil was still not able to digest what had actually happened. The deal, glitterati, media coverage, attention and a sudden feeling of heights, as if you have peaked the Everest or maybe further high, maybe the moon was palpable.

One drink after the other, a wonderful waterfront and a nice starry night made Rachel lose herself. As Neil went for a leak break, she spiked Neil's drink. Not that he wasn't really high, but she wanted to leave no stone unturned to get Neil naked. She was eyeing him and held a record that once she was high, then it was difficult for the one she was fond of to escape.

Neil blanked out after another drink. Rachel held him close and kissed his lips. That moment was enough for shutterbugs to appear from nowhere. By the time the cameras began to shoot in frenzy and unlimited excitement, Rachel had almost unzipped Neil and pushed her hand inside while riding on him for long smooches. There was no doubt that the news next day would be wickedly and wildly interesting. Neil had already suffered a near divorce situation not too long ago. He was in for another disaster. Rachel had no clue what was going on as she had passed out.

It was 6 a.m. when Gauri saw a bad dream. She knew it would just be 3 a.m. in Cape Town so she didn't want to call Neil. But she was so worried that she couldn't stop texting her man. She did that a couple of dozen times. Neil's phone did not show a delivery receipt. Out of anxiety, she called him on his phone. As she would have expected, his phone was switched off. She thought to herself if she was over-reacting. However, it was now not just the dream, but also the fact that the man who would never keep his phone off, was seemingly off the radar.

She finally called the reception desk. She was told that Neil had not returned to the hotel. Well, this was also unusual. She did not know who else to wake up. And it would be insane to call up or check with Rachel. Though the thought did strike her a couple of times, however it was ruled out for now. She breathed in and breathed out, and texted Mehr to ensure she had some comfort at this hour.

Her mom was sleeping in the next room, but she couldn't disturb her by knocking on her door. Gauri had been like that. Even when she and Neil faced the traumatic phases of their relationship, she was the last person to rope in the parents. And this was causing her nausea, so she ended up calling Mehr, who was deep asleep and hence had not responded to her text.

"Where the fuck is Neil, yaar? His phone is off and he isn't back at the hotel. Rachel is your friend. Call her."

"Calm down, Gauri! These panic attacks happen during pregnancy sometimes. I have seen this with few of my friends."

"I am a doctor and I know it. Call up Rachel, will you?"

Mehr had already dialled her number. It was ringing, but she wasn't picking up the phone.

"She must be asleep. Her phone is ringing. Let me check at the hotel."

The hotel line was busy. Suddenly Gauri hung up on Mehr as she attended to the call that apparently was from The Westin, Cape Town. She fumbled while holding the phone closer.

"Yes, tell me, quick!"

"Ma'am, Mr Neil had shared your details as the emergency contact and we had the direction to always give the information to you. May I quickly ask your date of birth for verification?"

"Sounds weird. My date of birth is 16th June 1983. Now can you tell me about his whereabouts, is he back?"

"So sorry, Mrs Gauri. It was our bad. He was back and I believe he is asleep. You can dial back at the hotel and I shall connect you to his room. And sorry once again. I apologize."

"No, that's fine. I am relieved."

Gauri called up the hotel though, to leave a voice message.

Ten minutes earlier, Neil had arrived at the hotel, completely sloshed. Rachel was holding him to keep him steady. They were dead drunk. He reached out to the reception asking for the room key. The staff mentioned to him about his wife's call. He got conscious immediately. Any news that sends shock waves through your body alerts you and that's what had happened. Neil asked this person to call Gauri in five minutes and asked him to lie to her. He couldn't let her worry at such a time.

Neil heard the voice message from his wife. In her voice, fear and even the sound of tears that were subsiding was clearly evident. In the voice, there was vulnerability. There was also happiness like she had found some hidden treasure. Above all, there was unlimited love and infinite care.

Baby, I was so worried about you. I saw a bad dream about us. I just woke up and called you and then the hotel. Then I called Mehr, and when I could not trace you, I sank. Please talk to me as soon as you hear this. I cannot live without you, Neil. We were better earlier. Please come back to me soon. I need you. Please… please Neil.

Neil heard this message about a couple of dozen times and recorded it in his phone.

"Damn you, Neil. Damn! You are an asshole. You almost fucked Rachel today and don't even remember what happened. Again you will blame the circumstances. There is nothing that can be done to you. Soon, you are going to be a father. Look at yourself! Look at what you are doing. Gauri deserves much better. Fix yourself and go back to her!"

He alerted himself. He knew exactly what needed to be done. Only until three more hours. As his life would change any way after the next three hours.

It was 7 a.m. The hotel staff was abuzz with activities. The sound of the morning alarm that was on recurring mode woke Neil up. He had no clue about the time. In half sleep dreamy mode, he got up and turned the television on. He checked his mobile phone. He checked for any further messages on the voice mail. That's what a guilty man does. He panics. He checks the news. He believes he will soon be in a spot.

"In a bizarre incident last night, billionaire Rachel from India slapped a camera man who was trying to take her picture while she was kissing her unnamed beau. This is not the first time Rachel has been involved in a controversy. Last year, she had publicly humiliated her ex-CEO who then went on record stating that she was only being vindictive. We are trying to contact Rachel and her office, however nobody is available for comment yet. When we contacted the photographer, he clearly told us that Rachel was in a compromising position on the beach which caught his attention. When he began to click, she hit him hard. More on this in some time. Next on the news update is growing sea food demand in the region and lack of supply…"

The news froze the blood inside Neil. He stood still and began to think of Gauri without a blink. He knew what he was into this time. For the next ten minutes, this still did not change, nor did his mind calm down. And he very well knew, because of the Indian connection, this would make headlines soon. The media in South Africa seemed out of control. The PR did not have any time to reach them or shut them up. Anything that would happen would only be reactive.

"Fuck! I need to talk to Rachel asap. She is the one who has made a mess."

Neil tried reaching out to Rachel, who apparently wasn't available in her room, nor on the phone. That was weird.

Rachel had stepped out to talk to her PR. However, the news had gone viral. Some of the local channels had stopped showing it, some even defended them stating that it was an act of the camera and hence not authenticated, and there were still the ones who would show it the the whole day long, making sure that people could not forget it.

What was feared the most just happened. Gauri called up Neil. The newswire was picked up by a few media channels and soon by some like Firstpost and India Today.

She straight away jumped to the point.

"Neil, what the hell is this now? This is like a deja vu to me. Why do women have to fall on you every time you and I get away. What is this, Neil? I need to know now…can you—"

Before Gauri could stop her bombardment of questions, Neil interrupted her.

"Exactly Gauri. My problem of trusting people bites me back again. I will explain everything to you. She spiked my drinks and I was caught by surprise. We stepped out after bagging the deal and I simply thought she would want to share something about business plans. I did not have the option to say no. It is that simple," said Neil breathlessly.

"You always have the option, Neil. You did not have to go to the beachside at eleven in the night with a woman who was seemingly drunk. Unless you had lost your senses and were in an inebriated state. Because only then you would run out of the option of saying no. And mister, I need no explanation. I want to address the media here as I have been bombarded with queries. I will handle them," retorted Gauri.

Neil wanted to gauge the situation and her reactions towards him. He treaded with caution.

"Gauri, you know you have been an angel in my life. Without your support, I would be nothing. And now we are going to be three soon. I have already prepared my resignation note. Thankfully, the terms and conditions and any hard coded legal clauses weren't embedded, so it would be easy that way. Booking my rerun flight. Coming into your arms soon," said Neil with a sigh of relief.

Gauri was least reactive. She felt like she was at the receiving end. She knew it would not be easy to convince the world that her husband was not an infidel. She knew that even if she was convinced with all the justification, there wouldn't be much she could do except send a note to the press and call on her friends and family to douse the fire. The fire that might take a really long time to die down. And the biggest fear that would run in the household was not to let the fire engulf this relationship.

The way Gauri was dealing with the situation was commendable. She neither displayed any of her insecurities or vulnerabilities before anyone, including Neil. Nor did she stick to the topic to the point of cribbing and crying. She was balanced and in complete control. She sent the email out to the media as a response to the questions.

My husband is completely innocent. Please do not fabricate him. Please do not write about him till you know the complete truth. Some amateur photographer sent these pictures and you have not even authenticated those. Maybe it is fake, or Rachel was up to something, or whatever it is, just leave us alone.

The press took the note of the statement and few channels in India ran the news, changing it in any way they pleased.

'Rachel lusted Neil with her charm?'

'Neil planning to wed Rachel later this year.'

'Neil's wife confirmed something is not good between the couple.'

'Another high profile couple spotted holidaying in Cape Town.'

Though Gauri had deliberately decided to not watch any of the news channels, there were many so-called friends who wouldn't let her escape the reality. She decided to go on a break with Mehr to avoid the inevitable. She had no interest whatsoever to go through the rigmarole.

Rachel was burning furiously. She was told about the news shown on the Indian channels. To add to it, the press in Cape Town was spicing it up further. She knew what needed to be done. She called up a few of her confidantes, got the PR active and blasted who she needed to. Adding to her wounds was the unceremonious exit of Neil, who left without a note or anything. She howled as this was completely unexpected. There was an email from Neil that simply shook her. It was her vs him now.

"Look, I don't care. Whatever money is needed. The media needs to know a few things across the world. Neil spiked my drink and I believe he even used rape drugs. I even tried reaching the cops. They came, but Neil has run away from the country. He knew he won't be spared and the punishment here might even be death sentence, and he wouldn't get any lawyer to fight his case. I am in a bad state. I will call my parents now, and am sending a note to all my employees right now. I have no time. The action needs to take place now."

Rachel changed her stance and turned vindictive. She was losing it.

She was supervising it all personally. A lot was at stake for her. She couldn't let it slip up at all. She could go to any extent to avoid any damage to her image. She was sure that she would come out of it and put all of the blame on Neil. Was it a temporary reaction or did she really mean to go all out against him? Would she try to stop him?

As time passed, there were ups and downs in the lives of the couple. Gauri was in her sixth month of pregnancy. Neil was serving a career break. He was working on something that he had been longing to do for a long time. Network security and digital transformation was on his mind. He had done some significant amount of work and was away from all distractions. The last few months had been extremely difficult for him, more so than anybody else. Rachel was trying to disturb his life in some form or the other, mostly indirectly. Without leaving a trace, but just a hint with Neil that it was her. She knew the man would not want to be embroiled in a controversy again and hence she could continue with her tactics. She wanted to gain his attention and try to get him back. Her efforts had been in vain, though. They never met again after the media episode, even though they did a lot to settle the dust. It was a different thing that Neil's image was tarnished. Also, he had become a little more secretive. And sometimes, Gauri would bring up the topic when she felt there was a need.

The last time both of them had a tiff was when Neil asked Gauri to move to Mumbai since the city offered them greater opportunities. She had unnecessarily dragged Rachel.

"Look Gauri, please understand, I am doing it all for us. Mumbai is the commercial capital of India. I have been there several times. Am quite familiar with the culture and also have a strong network there," reasoned Neil.

"The kind of work you are doing is more relevant in Bangalore. I cannot understand how Mumbai has become the technology hub of India? Or are you interested to go there because of a certain person?" replied Gauri.

"You know, a lot of companies and government sectors have their corporate offices in Mumbai. That is the reason. And I shall have an office in Bangalore as well. There is a big plan, Gauri. And you very well know that woman has no role in my life or ours," said Neil.

"Then why does she keep writing to you? Why does she? Why do you not confide in me? Why have you begun to hide things from me, Neil?" replied Gauri in anger.

"So you've started snooping on me now. That is simply not expected of you, Gauri. There was nothing relevant that I need to come and tell you. If I can handle things at my end, well then

I take care of them rather than bother you during this time when you need my care, love and nothing else."

Gauri walked towards Neil and held his hands, "*Kam se kam mera haath toh pakad lete.* You have been delivering all these lectures from such a distance."

"I am so sorry honey. I might have been far physically, but all this while, I was completely lost in you. Like completely. Can you promise me one thing today?"

"I know you will ask me that I should not doubt you ever. And that I've got to take care and let us do it all together," said Gauri exuding confidence.

"Haha, that would make it a typical husband-wife conversation. All you said is what we should do. But the promise I want from you today is that after our baby or twins are born, we will not stop making love."

"Is there a Viagra for women that can help overcome any fears in case I lose physical urge? If that is what you are hinting at?" smiled Gauri.

They carried on with the day and tried to reconcile any differences that had surfaced. A married couple can have fears at any point of their relationship. The fear of losing love, of losing the person or anything that would keep them distant. No matter what it is, everything can be taken care of with active communication. In the case of Neil and Gauri, one thing that was noticeable now was their level of communication. Since the incident with Drishti and Srinya had taken place, they were extremely conscious of this fact. Another thing that kept the couple going was that they would fight and then would kiss and make up. They now knew that relationships were not just about loving each other. They were about how stubborn you were to keep it going through rough times. That attitude of not giving up, being demanding, being crazily involved and saying to oneself everyday– "Let me see how I cannot be happy with my partner." That keeps the relationship going.

❖

It was the 2nd of July 2012. Neilakshi was born. That was the happiest day of their lives. Parenthood was the best feeling ever. The course of life would begin to change. The baby was adorable and Gauri could not stop looking at her. Families and friends kept sending their congratulatory messages.

In a few days, Neil started getting a lot of purchase orders for his firm, which was named NG Networks. Neilakshi was lucky for them. Their life turned about three hundred and sixty degrees. He hit a home run when a huge contract with Indian defence system was bagged by their company after defeating Rachel in the final round.

The last few days had been extremely hectic for the couple. Neil was travelling to and from Mumbai. Gauri was also in the last state of pregnancy. After Neilakshi was born, one thing that had become clear was the focus on parenting as well as establishing and growing their company.

Over the next few years, as life progressed, Neil went on to expand his company and shifted base to Mumbai to establish the headquarters. Gauri had also started another dental hospital there. As Neil continued to grow and get more work orders, he built a pattern of having certain rivalries.

In the meantime, Rachel was planning to get into Cuba to expand the construction business. She had reached the final two. The other was Neil.

Rachel did not want to lose this deal under any circumstances. She knew a simple, straight way might not do her any good. According to her, Neil was way too smart to come in her way yet again and grab this big deal as well.

She got the emails at NG enterprises hacked. There was no evidence that Neil's team could gather. The news did spread. It took a lot of time and effort for Neil and his company to regain their confidence. The one-sided attack from Rachel continued.

Despite all the adversities and challenges, Neil went on to soar, and continued to rise. From being one of the most influential men on the planet to being featured as the TIME's man of the year, the list of achievements was only growing longer.

Soon enough, it was planned that Neil and Gauri would travel to Cuba together. They were invited by Alicia and Sreedhar for the book launch. It was the true story of the couple. They had also planned to spend some additional time to visit the places that were earmarked for construction of temples. It was decided to begin the official work after they would attend the Aerosmith concert. It brought back many memories.

"Neil, it's the best feeling to be here and watch our favourite band Aerosmith at the place where we did years ago. A lot has changed, but we still remain the same," said Gauri.

"Yes, Gauri. Our life has always been adventurous. There have been so many ups and downs, but no matter what, we have stayed strong."

After the concert was over, the couple decided to go to the village for the food festival. They wanted to have a good time sans security.

On their way from the stadium to the village, they stopped the car and took pictures. Neil sent the pictures to Tom. Neil took the steering wheel from Gauri as she sent more pictures to Tom. She saw a couple of pictures of Neil and Rachel together in his phone, and she. lost it. It came as a rude shock to her. An argument began. It reached a point where Gauri asked Neil to let her return the next day. She was adamant and Neil was saddened. She would not listen to him even though he was trying to explain his side of the story. Suddenly, the car lost control and it hit a tree with full force.

❖

Present day

Neil had gained complete consciousness now. There was a massive security cover provided to the couple as they were kept in the minister's house.

Gauri had sought a day's time to themselves from the cops. She reached out to Neil and held his hands.

"Neil, I am so sorry. All of this has happened because of me. I hurt you, my love. You kept on saying and explaining about that photograph and I simply did not listen to you," Gauri started off by apologizing.

"Gauri, can you calm down? In the last so many hours, it is you who has seen all the pain. I have only been sleeping." Neil smiled.

Gauri could not control her emotions. She cried holding her husband tight. The last forty-eight hours had been literally insane.

The world has closed the pages of day
They're now embracing slumber,
Look how the Sun for the world has set
And watch how the Sun of night has risen,
This blanket of starry bright twinkles,
A curtain embedded gems that sparkles,
These dim lights
And this fervent twilight,
We look up to a sky that is brushed
Yes, it's painted black, my darling.
These roofs of blue space have been dipped
In the palette with hues of the night dark
But then, this canvas of nightfall
Has pearls of love that you gifted me
Love has struck my chords of essence
I hear the song of your fragrance
in my soul, in my substance
In my existence
Be the knight of darkness
And I be your lady of fondness!

Media ran the news of crackdowns at the cartel key places. There were several raids being conducted. Juan came down heavily on all the folks who have had linkages with the cartel in the past and those who have been convicted at some point.

The men who had come to attack the oldies and the couple were traced to the old gang of Santiago. He was nabbed along with his men.

Juan ran the interrogation personally. Santiago was not easy to break. To be in this state was not the first for him. He clearly denied having any link whatsoever and mentioned that those men did not work for him anymore.

It was for Juan to find out who ratted out. The information about the victimised couple's stay of address at Artemisa was only known to Carlos and Santiago. Carlos informed Juan. So it was a simple equation to decipher that Santiago tipped off and hence the specific attack took place. That also meant that the people who came to kill them the second time around never wanted them to be alive. They belonged to the same gang that attempted on their life the first time. Juan sent Santiago to his men and directed them to interrogate in their own way and find the truth from him.

Now was the turn for Gauri to identify the attackers. Their bodies lay in the morgue. It was tough for her at first, but she had no choice.

She could recognize one of them, however was not certain. For Juan, that was good enough. He was very clear when he conversed with Gauri.

"Ma'am, you don't worry at all. We shall find out the perpetrators soon enough. You are safe now."

"Yes, thank you. The government has been extremely supportive."

"Okay, now I just want to ask you a few questions, if you allow."

"Sure, please go ahead!"

"Do you have any animosity with anyone in this town? I know it is very idiotic for me to ask you, yet if you could tell anything?"

"Not that we remember. However, we were getting threatening letters for quite some time in the name of Isabella."

Juan got up and showed the number plate to Gauri. She was astonishingly surprised to see that the number plate had the same font and name as it was carried in all the handwritten letters as well as in the email that Neil received recently.

"This is unbelievable. What the heck… I cannot digest it," Gauri began to pant heavily.

Juan offered her water. She put her forehead down in utter disbelief.

Juan continued. "Thanks for being cooperative. Is there anything else you would like to share?"

"I don't know what all to say, as you can imagine that in business, you have normal rivalries. So did we do. Neil had a spat with a billionaire named Rachel, if you have heard her name. She runs a company by the name Trust Cements and Steel Pvt Ltd. Recently, she lost a contract to our company. We won the bid and were going for a deal worth more than 200 million USD. But I don't think she can kill anyone or think of planning all this. Anyway, that's all that I can think of," Gauri continued.

"Okay, we will get the investigation details on Rachel and few other folks soon. CBI has assured us of the information any moment. A team is also landing from India anytime now. Let's see what we get. Thanks a lot ma'am. I shall keep you in the loop," beamed Juan with confidence.

A press release was issued by Juan:

'We have made some excellent progress in the case. I have directed my teams to work on something more specific now. I cannot reveal everything at this stage, but I assure you that we will close this case in the next 4 hours. Thank you.'

❖

At David More's residence

It was all quiet, very quiet, except the two talking in the corner of their room. Their staff was sent out. David and Arya were engaged in some serious discussion.

"Arya, when you had told me how this man had made your life hell, I had decided that day to take him down. It is that simple."

"David, since when have you started taking decisions on my behalf? Do you have any idea what you have done? Was our life any less complicated earlier that you thought of killing these folks?" said Arya who was still reeling under the shock.

"Nobody would be able to reach us. Nobody. Yes, it is true that I was not expecting it to become such a big news, honestly."

"David, where are the cars that were used by your goons?"

"The cars belonged to Carl, and have now been trashed and the men belonged to Freddie."

"The world knows that Freddie used to work for you."

"Not anymore. And he has already moved to Russia. And so has Carl."

"I am shit scared, David. The cops will be here any moment. This man Juan has announced that he will solve it in four hours."

"They will nab people like Santiago, which I have been told he already has. In four hours, all they will do is frame someone and make him admit that they committed the crime. That's all."

While David admitted to have plotted the crime entirely, yet he had left no trace that could roll back to him as any sort of evidence. Arya was inquisitive in knowing everything. David did not hide anything from her. Though he only confessed to her at this stage. People go crazy in love. Then there are some who lose their sanity. David was one of the insane kinds. Who on earth would even think of hatching a plot that was based on a revenge for something that happened to a girl in college? And now the husband of that girl is the perpetrator of a crime that involved passion and a giant country like India. If he were caught, there would be no less than a life time imprisonment for him.

Arya was therefore keen in knowing everything so that if needed she could help her husband. The theory of saving a criminal meant being a party to crime did not apply in this case. She was the wife.

When Neil bagged the contract of business deals in Cuba, it was David's land that government was eyeing. He ran his drug cartel in the garb of religious activities. When Neil spoke with the government of Cuba that he was keen in building temples here, David got to know about it from his sources. The hatred that David carried for Neil turned into a full-fledged determination to wipe him out. However, he made the plan thoughtfully.

He figured everything about Neil's past and present and his friendships and hostilities. He understood that Rachel was the weak link in the story. He created an alibi and a shell company in the name of Isabella that was operating from Russia. He hired a professional who was called V, in Moscow, who worked under cover for him. He created a maze by having multiple people work for them for money laundering. Coincidentally, Rahul Sood was one of them.

David siphoned off his funds to this company in Moscow that kept him afloat. He had been in money laundering to turn drug money into clean money so there was nothing new in that. What was new was Isabella and using it to send money to Freddie to give shape to the murder of the couple. The script went awry.

At that point, David knew that Rachel was extremely upset with Neil after losing the contract to him. She was miles away from reaching her goal of a billion dollar which was a matter of pride for her. V reached out to Rachel and told her he would get her more than 200 million dollar worth business deals in Cuba, provided she makes a payment of a few million dollars to the company in Moscow. Rachel was aware it was an illegal transaction as she ran a business empire herself, but she got blinded by the 200 million dollar business commitment.

For David, it was the perfect shot. It would be Rachel's money that would be used to fund Freddie to kill Neil and Gauri. The transactions would only happen via Moscow. Nothing would trace back to David or Arya.

On the other hand, Freddie also played smart. He used the same Russian connection to incite Santiago into finding the couple. The second time when the attack took place, the attackers would lead to Santiago, who would have nothing much to substantiate that he was not behind the crime.

The maths changed heavily after the prize money to find the couple alive was bumped up to 2 million USD.

CBI had finished its investigation and sent the detailed report to Juan and the ministers in Cuba, as well as relevant folks in India.

Dhanya had landed in Cuba and was in several discussions with the local crime bureau.

She decided to first meet Carlos.

"Hi Dhanya, I am so sorry I let you down. I could not do my best on the case."

"Carlos, it is fine, but an officer of your stature was moved out of this investigation. May I know why?"

Carlos broke down completely. Dhanya was shocked to see a tough cop go through this emotional upheaval. She assured him that she shall maintain complete confidentiality. Carlos thanked her and spoke softly.

"They are nasty people, Dhanya. They bloody blackmailed me. I got calls from Russia and even Venezuela, threatening me that if I pursue this case, they will show my videos to my family. Now please don't ask me what videos. I was no saint at one point. But now I am a family man. I am sorry Dhanya. I am extremely sorry. I am shattered," sobbed Carlos.

Dhanya held his hands. She then gave him a warm hug.

"Nobody is a saint. But a man who admits his sin and confides is far superior than even a saint. In my view, my respect for you has only gone up. You must stand tall like a man. And one thing you promise me, you will tell your wife everything. You will be liberated after that."

Carlos had never thought that Dhanya would react in such a peaceful way.

"I shall remain indebted to you, young lady. And you know, I believe in Karma. I shall seek forgiveness from my wife and Lord Krishna."

Dhanya smiled and left for her immediate next steps. She met with Neil and Gauri.

Tom and Mehr also arrived with Neilakshi. The atmospherics turned magnificent. Their joy knew no bound. Alicia and Sridhar were ecstatic as they saw how things had changed in the last day-and-a-half.

Gauri was completely engaged, talking about whatever had taken place. In some time, the folks left the spot to meet the cops, leaving the couple and Neilakshi together.

Neil held Gauri's and Neilakshi's hand and remained quiet for sometime. Gauri reciprocated and only looked in his eyes. They both kissed their daughter.

At the office of the Crime Bureau, Juan came out and made the statement to the media

'I am extremely pleased with everyone in my team who have worked relentlessly to solve this high profile case. We are preparing the chargesheet and shall appeal to the court for capital punishment. Santiago has admitted to play a role in plotting the murder. There is some link to Russia here. The prime motive of Santiago was to make some quick money that he was offered via transfer into his bank account. The account was traced back to Russia. Prima facie, it appears to be a case where there are certain drug cartels who might have been linked to the rivals of the owner of NG Networks. There is no other reason we see at this point. The investigations shall continue from our end. But let me assure you, we are safe here. They are all safe here. My direction to the cops in my team is to ensure that all the mafia is shut down and we only focus on constructive activities. Also, Neil and Gauri have decided to give the 2 million dollar reward to the old couple who saved their lives. Thank you very much. I am now ready to take on your questions.'

Juan sent a powerful message not only to his country, but the world over. Of course, the masterminds of the crime were far from being caught and might never be, yet, there was some breakthrough according to him.

While in India, Rachel was arrested; here in Cuba, David More was roaming Scott free.

❖

Over the next two days, Neil planned to visit the lands that the government had confirmed to him for building the Krishna temple. He was accompanied by a couple of ministers.

"Hi Mr More," said one of the ministers.

"Hi sir, so nice to meet you, please come inside," said David.

Neil was slightly away and was looking around along with the other minister. He was trying to catch a wifi signal to WhatsApp Gauri as the local network signal was weak. The wifi name showed as Isabella.

As Neil walked in, the minister introduced, "Hi Neil, meet this very lovely human being, Mr David More and his equally lovely wife, Mrs Arya More."

By the same author

MESSED UP! BUT ALL FOR LOVE

Neil is a senior executive working with a leading brand name and his wife Gauri is a dentist running her own clinic. They are a loving and doting young married couple, living a life of comfort in posh suburban Gurgaon. Neil's fitness consultant Srinya seems to be stirring some trouble in their lives, though.

Drishti is a TV news anchor and journalist and her husband Somesh, a top cop. They are bored of their mundane busy lives, until a chance meeting with Neil and his friends in Cuba that changes everything.

To add sanity and madness to their lives are the funny and mysterious set of friends - Tom, Jerry, James, Mehr and Antriksha.

The havoc ensues when Drishti gets abducted and Neil is framed for it. Gauri finds out some bitter truths and leaves Neil. But what really is the truth?

When facts finally surface, we will know how much these lives are *Messed Up! But All for Love.*

LOST IN LOVE

Neil had many questions related to his life. Having suffered a total eclipse of the heart, dumped by Arya, he had nowhere to go. He was completely shattered. Till one fine day, when his friend Gauri, who had a crush on Neil ever since her childhood, comes into his life and they begin their journey of love, romance, fantasy and fairy tales. Not for long, as their world comes crashing with a tragic, life-turning event. This is a heart-wrenching romance thriller that is bound to move you and hit your soul as you take a plunge and get *Lost in Love*.